Gravel
Road™

Sometimes we find ourselves on a gravel road, not sure of how we got there or where the road leads. Sharp stones pellet the unprotected. And the everyday wear and tear sears more deeply.

Nasreen

I knock on my brother's door. His rap music is so loud, I'm sure he can't hear me. I pound louder. "Jaffar! Open up!"

The volume goes down. He opens his door a crack and glares at me. "What?"

I clear my throat. He never lets me forget that he's older than me. That I'm just his little sister. "I need your help," I say.

He glances at the pamphlets I'm holding. "College brochures? You're only a junior."

"I know. I'm starting early."

He rolls his eyes. "Of course you are."

"I don't have a clue where to go or how to apply."

"Okay." He sighs. "Come in." He takes the pamphlets from me. Shakes his head as he glances at the first cover. "Harvard? No way."

"Why not?"

He fingers through the rest. "Cal Tech? MIT? Stanford? Nasreen, these are all top universities."

"So?"

"So our parents aren't rich."

"Mr. Clarke said I can apply for scholarships."

"I applied for scholarships and where am I going?"

"But you want to be an accountant. State college is perfect for you."

"Oh, that's right," he says. "You're the brains in the family." He shoves the brochures back at me.

"I just want your advice."

"And who advised me? No one. Because I'm the oldest and did it myself. Go online and figure it out." He turns his music up.

I leave, closing the door behind me.

Back in my bedroom, I set the brochures on my desk. I think about asking my parents. But they know nothing about American colleges. As I sink into my beanbag chair, I imagine all the kids at school whose parents will be helping them decide which colleges to apply to. Parents who aren't from Pakistan and get confused by American rules and language.

Taking a deep breath, I pull my calculus book onto my lap. I enter a few numbers into my graphing calculator and try to ignore Jaffar's loud music thumping through our shared wall.

By ten o'clock, my homework is

finished. I wish I had more. I start thinking about school tomorrow. The familiar knot ties in my stomach.

Mom pokes her head around my door. "It's time for bed, Nasreen," she says in Punjabi.

"I know," I mutter back in English.

"What's wrong?"

"Nothing."

She stares at me a moment. Then she says, "Good night," closing my door.

My parents have a hard enough time just getting by in this country. I decided a long time ago I wouldn't be one of the things they had to worry about. Just a year and a half. A year and a half and I won't have to deal with the students at Arondale High School anymore.

It's a little too early when I get to the bus stop. I lean against a tree, away from the others, trying to make myself invisible.

When the bus pulls up, I stand at the back of the crowd, my jaw tight, my eyes lowered. Guys jostle and shove each other as they get on.

We're one of the first stops. That's good because I can always find an empty seat. Not so good because it's twenty more minutes until we get to school.

The bus starts moving. From the back seat, Samantha shouts, "Hey, I just figured out why she wears that stupid scarf!"

"Why?" her friend Melody asks, setting her up.

"To protect her head from bird poop. I wish *I* had one."

They laugh.

The bus driver glares at them in the rearview mirror and shakes her head. Samantha and her friends won't say anything else, or they'll get written up. I shrink into my seat anyway. At the next stop, Kyle Spencer sits behind me. My shoulders rise protectively around my neck.

"Hi, Nasty Nasreen," he whispers through my *hijab*. I lean away from him, curling my fingers into fists. I review math equations in my head.

At the next stop, someone sits next to me. No one *ever* shares my seat. Great. What do I have to put up with now?

CHAPTER 2

Mia

I wake up in the middle of the night sweating. It's so hot in here! My bed is layered with three blankets and a quilt. I throw the quilt off. Jump up and pull back the frilly curtain covering the window. The window doesn't lift open like the one in Mom's apartment. It cranks. And the crank isn't budging. God, I'm about to suffocate! Then I notice a lever. Lift it up. Turn the crank until the window gapes wide. It's February in Iowa and freezing outside. I don't care. It feels good. I breathe in a lungful of crisp air.

As I crawl back into bed, I remember

the dream I had before I woke up. As always, Mom was in it. I don't remember the details, just the feeling. Fear. Lots of fear. Which makes sense, because I am afraid. Of starting a new school in the morning. Of living with my grandmother, who I hardly know. Of being sent to foster care if this doesn't work out.

Now the room is too cold. I curl into a ball and shiver instead of closing the window. Why bother? I'm not going back to sleep anyway.

At six o'clock I smell coffee. Then bacon. Damn, is she going to cook breakfast every morning? Saturday was pancakes. Yesterday, waffles. I get up. Shower. Stand in front of the closet. Whatever white kids wear in the burbs, I'm sure I don't have it. I throw on my ripped jeans, black T, gray hoodie.

I walk into the kitchen.

Gram smiles at me from the stove

where she's scrambling eggs. "Good morning, Mia. Have a seat." With her straight gray hair, pale skin, and blue eyes, it's hard to believe we're related.

The table is set with plates, silverware. Glasses of orange juice. Toast on a serving platter. Butter and jam. "You don't have to do all of this," I say as I pull out a chair. "I'm fine with a bowl of cereal."

"I know. I just...." She shrugs her shoulders. Her smile wavers, and she looks like she might cry. She turns back to the frying pan.

Wow. Awkward much?

She dishes up our plates with eggs. Sits across from me. Lowers her eyes and clasps her hands on the table. "Bless this food, O Lord. Bless this house and those who dwell within it. Amen."

"Amen," I repeat softly. I think that's what I'm supposed to say. Mom and I never said grace.

She sips her coffee. "Are you nervous about your first day of school?"

Duh. Of course I am. But I've noticed Gram is on the fragile side. I don't want to upset her. So I say, "A little."

"You'll do fine." She pats my hand. Gives me a reassuring smile. Her dimples remind me of Mom. I eat enough to be polite. Then I head to the bus stop. Gram pointed it out Saturday on our grand tour of Arondale.

I count eight other kids waiting at the corner. As soon as they realize I'm waiting with them, they stop talking and stare. I stand back a ways. Try to blend in with the scenery. The bus pulls up. I get on last. Taking a deep breath, I look down the aisle. I'm not used to school buses. But I rode a lot of public buses in Chicago, and I know better than to sit in the back. That's where all the bad crap happens.

All I see are white faces. Then, surprise, about four seats back I glance brown skin like mine, just a little lighter. She's wearing a blue headscarf that hides her hair and forehead. She's staring at her hands. I hope she's not saving the seat for a friend, because it looks like home to me.

Nasreen

I notice the bus has gone quiet. Of course I think it's because of me. The person who sat down is going to say or do something to humiliate me. Everyone will have their morning laugh. But when nothing happens, I glance over. I see worn, faded jeans with holes in the knees. Above that is a gray hoodie, and then a girl's face. She has light brown skin. Dark brown hair frizzes down to her shoulders.

She looks over. "Hey," she says and gives me a small smile.

"Hi," I say back. Embarrassed for staring, I lower my eyes.

Now I know what the quiet was about. Everyone was gawking at the new girl. The new black girl. She'll be the only one at Arondale High. Just like I'm the only Muslim. Part of me feels sorry for her. Part of me wishes she'd sat somewhere else. I don't need the added attention. Then I quickly scold myself for thinking so selfishly.

I look out the window. Five days to the end of the week. Fifteen weeks to the end of the year.

My first period is chemistry. Like in most of my classes, I sit toward the front. I learned that lesson the hard way in middle school. For some reason, classmates' feet kept finding their way into aisles as I walked by. Sitting in front isn't always safe either. Mrs. Jamison is late this morning. The room is noisy. Raucous. Something hits the back of my hijab and clatters to the floor. It sounds like a pencil. I hear laughter.

"Hey, can you return that please?" I recognize Felicia Norris's voice. There's more laughter. I don't acknowledge her. And I don't retrieve her pencil.

French is second period. It's relatively peaceful this morning. Then I have the highlight of my day, AP Calculus. No one teases me in this class. But I keep to myself because it's what I'm used to. Plus, I'm never sure who I can completely trust.

I'm just pulling out my textbook when I notice the room has gone quiet. I look up. The girl from the bus is standing next to the teacher. At first I think she must be in the wrong room. But she shows her class schedule to Mr. Humphrey. He nods and says, "Sit anywhere."

She ambles to a desk in the back. Okay, I admit it. I'm surprised. To begin with, there are only eighteen of us in AP

Calculus. Just three girls. And except for Melvin Cho and me, everyone is white. And she looks so … I don't know. Urban, I guess. And then I realize I'm making assumptions. I hate it when people make them about me. Like that I'm a terrorist. Or that I hate Christians. Or that all Muslim women are oppressed. It's silly, but I feel like I should apologize to her.

Class starts. Mr. Humphrey says, "Care to introduce yourself?"

The girl shrugs. She shoves her hands into her hoodie pockets and mumbles, "Mia Ellis."

"What were you working on at your old school?"

"Derivatives."

"We've just begun integrals. You'll need to do a little extra work to catch up. Okay, Mia?"

She nods and thumbs through her textbook.

She doesn't say anything the rest of class.

After class, I'm at my locker getting my lunch. I see the top of Mia's curly head bobbing down the hallway. She stops where the math-science hallway intersects with the main corridor. She looks around, clearly confused.

I step up next to her. She's a little taller than me, maybe five foot seven. I'm not sure why I consider reaching out. Maybe because she sat next to me on the bus. Maybe because she's different, like me. "Do you need directions?" I ask.

She jumps a little. Then she looks over. "Yeah. The cafeteria?"

"Ah, the lunchroom."

"Is that what you call it here?"

I nod. "I'll show you if you like."

She hesitates. I can tell she's glancing at my hijab, trying not to be obvious about it. I can also tell she's making assumptions about me. Now we're even.

"Um, okay," she says. "That would be great."

I start walking. "You like math?" I ask.

"Yeah, it's fun. Hard, though."

"Yes, it can be."

Behind us I hear, "Hey, Muslim bitch. Who's your new friend?"

It's Samantha. I don't turn around.

"Muslim bitch, I'm talking to you."

My shoulders stiffen. I don't know what to do. If I were alone, I'd walk away as quickly as I could. But being with Mia, I feel embarrassed. Like I should be brave. Do something. Say something.

Suddenly, Mia stops walking. She spins around and says with a smile, "Hi. I'm Mia."

Samantha, Melody, and Rachel look Mia up and down.

"Who let you into the suburbs?" Samantha asks.

"I don't know. Who let you into the human race?"

Samantha stands there a few seconds. I can tell she's wondering what she's up against. "Are you a Christ hater too?"

"Not the last time I checked."

Samantha sneers. She and her friends walk between us, bumping us with their elbows.

"Wow, rough crowd," Mia says after they've left. "And here I thought people with lawns and barbecues would be mellow."

My jaw is hanging open. I can't believe how she just handled those girls. It makes me feel all the more cowardly.

"They been doing this to you for a while?" Mia asks.

I nod.

She sighs. "I hear ya. Try being an A student where a good education isn't exactly valued." Then she asks, "So ... what's your name again? I heard the teacher say it in class, but I don't remember. Sorry."

"That's okay. I'm Nasreen." We start walking again.

"Nasreen," she repeats. "That's pretty. So you're Muslim?"

"Yes. But I don't hate Christ."

She snickers. "Yeah. I didn't think so."

We've reached the entrance to the lunchroom and stop. "Here it is," I say.

"Aren't you going in?" she asks.

"No. I bring my lunch."

"Oh." She takes a deep breath. "So how many other jerks do I need to watch out for?"

"Many. If you like, I'll point them out to you sometime."

With a perfect Valley Girl voice she says, "Like, that would be totally awesome."

I smile.

She adds, "Though I have a feeling they'll be revealing themselves soon enough."

"Yes. That's very likely."

As I'm leaving, I tell her, "From what I hear, you should avoid the meatloaf."

"Got it. Thanks." Mia disappears into the lunchroom.

I take my lunch and eat alone outside.

CHAPTER 4

Mia

My first morning on the school bus. It's practically silent when I walk down the aisle. Either kids here are quiet and well behaved or I've shocked them. My guess is the latter. Maybe they've never seen a real live black person before. Even the girl with the headscarf is checking me out. I think, really? *You're* gawking? And then I feel bad for thinking that. Look at what she has to put up with. Does her religion make her wear that thing? Or maybe her parents? It can't possibly be voluntary. So I just smile and say hi. Maybe I'll kill everyone with kindness. That's a strategy.

This is not the first new school I've ever started. So I've got experience going for me. Mom and I moved around a lot, though we always stayed in cities. First New York, then Chicago. She'd get hyped about one scheme or another. She was going to start a restaurant. Then a chain of Laundromats. We'd make millions. Her mania was infectious, and I always got caught up in it. Then I'd get just as caught up in her disappointment when she crashed. We never got out of cheap apartments, bad neighborhoods.

I take a deep breath. Don't want to think about my past. Don't want to think about her.

The bus rumbles into the school parking lot. I can still feel people's eyes on my back, trying to figure me out. Fine. Have fun.

Once inside, I head to the school office to get my class schedule. The secretary stares at me, then squints at the printout. "Excuse me," she says with a cold smile. "I'll be right back." She disappears into a back room. I hear her talking to someone.

A man in a suit marches out. "Hello, Mia! I'm Principal Willems. Welcome to Arondale High." He sticks his hand out.

I shake it.

"You're transcripts haven't arrived yet. We just want to make sure we haven't made a mistake with your classes. Your grandmother signed you up for AP Calculus?"

"Yeah," I say.

"That's an Advanced Placement class."

"I know."

"You were taking AP Calculus at your old school?" He looks at another form. "Jefferson High in Chicago?"

"Yes."

He smiles. "Okay." Hands me the schedule. "We're delighted you're with us,

Mia. Let me know if you have any questions. Or if I can help in any way. My door is always open."

The secretary nods in agreement.

"Okay," I say. "Thanks." I start to walk out. Study my list of classes. First period is government, room B211. Huh. Where is that? I don't have a clue. So I turn to ask them. But they're both gone. Wow. Thanks for the help, guys. Even Jefferson had a student helper walk me to my first class.

Sighing, I look around the main hallway. It takes a while, but I finally find the B hall. I open the door and walk into the middle of class. Feel like a vampire at a werewolf convention. The teacher eyes me. "Yes?" she says.

I explain I'm a new student. She tells me to take an empty seat.

It goes like that the rest of the morning—me getting to class late because I don't know where the rooms are. Teachers staring. Kids staring.

In calculus, even the girl I sat next to on the bus stares.

First days sure suck.

After math is lunch, which is both good and bad. Good, because I'm starving and hoping the cafeteria has better food than at my old school. Bad, because of that whole where-should-I-sit thing. My goal is in the back, alone. Just me and my pizza.

I'm at the main corridor. Wondering where the heck I might find said cafeteria. When I hear, "Do you need directions?" It's the girl with the headscarf. Which I probably stare at a beat too long again. I promise myself to stop doing that.

She kindly walks with me to the *lunchroom*. (Good to know it's not a cafeteria.) We have a run-in with three girls in the hallway. I feel sorry for Nasreen. That's her name. She's obviously been putting up with these snarky bitches for a long time. I hope they don't become problems for me, though my Spidey sense tells me they will.

Confrontation over, Nasreen and I part ways. This saddens me a bit. She's a math geek like me. I would have welcomed her company. As it is, I take a deep breath, probably my hundredth of the day so far. Stand in line at the lunchroom counter. Feel the stares. Hear the whispers.

I really stick out here. Like a red zit on a white chin. It's kind of funny, in a way. I get the urge to say "Boo!" to the kid in line behind me. Just to see his eyes bug out. But I don't. The queue moves slowly. Deciding to at least make an attempt at friendly, I talk to the girl in front of me. "Do they have pizza?" I ask.

"Yes," she says, turning slightly but not meeting my eyes. "Usually."

"Is the meatloaf really that bad?"

"I … I don't know." She shrugs. "I like it." Before she faces front, she wraps her fingers tightly around her wallet and pulls it to her side. Like, what, I'm going to steal it?

Really?

I close my eyes a second. Take deep breath number one hundred and one.

I spot an empty seat far in the back. As I walk between the tables, I try to ignore the stares. The silenced conversations. I'm a novelty. And like all shiny new things, they quickly lose their luster. That's what I'm hoping for anyway.

CHAPTER 5

Nasreen

In seventh-period study hall, I pull the college brochures out of my backpack. I want to make a decision soon. I hear a familiar voice and look up. It's Mia. She's talking to Mrs. Belcher. I still feel embarrassed about what happened in the hallway with Samantha and her friends before lunch. But I'm glad Mia and I are sharing another class. I like her. It's been a long time since I've smiled at school.

She sits in the last row. I'm in my usual seat in the front. I look for kids back there who might harass me. I don't see any of the usual suspects. Grabbing my things, I move to the empty desk next to hers.

"Are you surviving your first day?" I ask her.

"Barely," she says. "The pizza has been the highlight so far." She opens her backpack. "What's a nerdy girl like you doing in study hall? I figured you'd have some exotic elective. Like the physics of basket weaving or something."

I laugh. "I don't need more units. And I like getting a head start on my homework. Why did you choose study hall?"

"I'm taking a psych class. That's enough elective for me." She looks at my desk. "That doesn't look like homework."

"No. I'm trying to figure out which colleges to apply to."

"Why not all of them?" Mia opens her calculus book.

"Because applications are expensive."

"Oh. I just assumed since you live in Arondale … " Her voice trails off.

"That we have money?" I say. "We did, once. My father had a job in Des Moines as a computer programmer. Then he got laid off. Now he's a gardener. My mother is a nurse's aide."

"Oh," she says.

Did I just share too much personal information? I'm not used to talking about myself. Changing the subject, I say, "There are so many good engineering schools. But I think I've narrowed it down." I hold up three of the pamphlets.

Mia takes them from me. "Man, I would love to go to any of these. But I wouldn't know where to begin." She looks wistfully at one of the covers. "I can't go without getting scholarships. I'll have to apply for those too. It all seems kind of impossible, you know? Like, *me*? Going to a university? I have a feeling I'll just keep putting it off and end up at a community college."

She hands the brochures back. I put them in my backpack. "Sometimes I feel the same way." I take out my chemistry homework. Without thinking, I say, "Would you like to research colleges together?" I instantly regret asking. Of course she wouldn't.

She tilts her head. "Sure. Where? When?"

I can't help smiling. "I don't know. At my house? This Saturday?"

"Hey," Taylor Carter twists in his seat and glares at us. "Will you two shut up?"

My cheeks warm with embarrassment. That's not a complaint I've heard before.

Saturday, Mom and I are doing laundry in the basement. She grimaces when she sees my hijab. "So she's not Muslim?"

"No."

Mom folds a bath towel in half, then folds it again. "Is she staying for dinner?"

"I didn't ask. Is it okay if she does?" I close the lid of the washer and press the On button.

I hear her loud sigh even over the sound of water sloshing into the machine.

"Mom, there are no Muslim kids at school to choose from."

She sets the towel on top of the stack. "All right. Fine. I'm looking forward to meeting Mia."

"Good. Thanks."

The doorbell rings as I'm crossing the living room with the towels. "Shoot." I set them on the couch and open the door.

Mia is standing on the porch with a laptop under her arm. "Hi," she says, stepping inside.

I look down. "Um. You need to take off your shoes."

She freezes in the entryway. "What?"

"Your shoes. They're not allowed inside."

"Oh." She steps on the heels of her sneakers and pulls her feet out. "Are socks okay?"

"As long as they don't smell."

She looks at me.

I smile. "I'm kidding. Muslim joke. Come in."

I pick up the towels. "Follow me. My room is this way."

I stuff the towels in the linen closet, and we go to my room. "Are you okay if we sit on the floor? I don't think there's space for both of us at my desk." I point at the beanbag chair. "You can sit there."

She does, almost tipping over. "Whoa!" she yelps, flailing her arms.

I laugh as she rights herself and squishes down into the chair. Once she's settled in, she says, "Ooh, I love this thing. I want one."

I grab my laptop and sit on the floor next to her with my back against the wall. "So where shall we start? MIT?"

"Really? Wow. Sure. Why not?" She turns on her computer and glances at me as she waits for it to boot up. "Can I ask you something? It's personal."

"Sure, I guess."

"Your headscarf. You have to wear it all the time?"

I hesitate. People rarely understand when I explain about my religion. They like to argue. Judge. But I think Mia is truly curious. "No. Not in front of my family. And it's called a hijab."

"So if I wasn't here, you wouldn't be wearing your … hijab?"

"That's right. I don't know you very well. You might describe my hair to men you know. And that would be immodest."

"It's about modesty, then?"

"And self-respect. I feel good when I

wear it. Like I'm honoring my faith. So if you were feeling sorry for me, you don't need to."

Mia nods. "Okay. I won't." She looks at her computer screen and takes a deep breath. "Watch out, MIT. Nasreen and Mia are in the house!"

I laugh. It's hard to believe I just had an open and rational conversation about my religion with someone from school.

We finish researching two colleges and take a break. I grab soft drinks from the kitchen. When I return, Mia is still focused on her computer.

"I thought we were taking a break," I say.

"We are. I'm checking out my online stuff."

"Oh. I started a Facebook page. But I never check it." I don't tell her I only use my account to keep track of my extended family. That would sound so lame.

She laughs at the screen. "Delia is a psycho." Mia holds her laptop at an angle so I can see. There's a photo of a black girl leaping off the hood of a car. Her arms and legs are outstretched. She's grinning crazily.

"Your friend?" I ask.

"Yeah. My only real friend." She pulls the computer back and starts typing.

While she's busy, I decide to check my Facebook page. When I do, I wish I hadn't.

CHAPTER 6

Mia

So I'm having a fine time at Nasreen's looking at college websites. She's pretty open about her religion, which I think is cool. I didn't know a thing about Islam. That stuff about the headscarf is interesting. Hijab. I thought she wore it because she had to, not because she wanted to. Personally, I wouldn't wear anything that brings me more attention. But if it makes her feel closer to God or whatever, I can't argue with that. (And I won't tell her this, but there are no men in my life to describe her to.)

I'm just finishing writing a comment to a crazy photo that Delia, my friend from Chicago, posted. Next to me, Nasreen gasps. I look over. She's staring at her computer, her mouth open.

"What is it?" I ask. Something is definitely wrong.

She doesn't say anything. Just keeps reading her screen. Then she buries her face in her hands. She's crying.

"Nasreen," I say. "What?"

She shoves her computer toward me. I pick it up and take a look at the screen. It's her Facebook page. Her last post was six months ago. I can't believe the messages:

Raghead.
Go back to Iraq, stupid cow.
You don't deserve to live.

There's an ugly sexual reference that makes my stomach twist. I scroll up.

Someone posted a message just yesterday:

Enjoying your new black bitch? Why don't you move to Africa with her. Keep America white and raghead free.

Heat rises to my face. I want to throw the computer across the room. "Holy crap," I mutter. "Is it okay if I close this page?"

She nods.

I close the lid and set the computer on her lap. She presses her fingers against her eyes. "I'm sorry for crying," she says.

"Don't be. Those comments are disgusting."

She jumps up and grabs a tissue. Blows her nose. "I had no idea those were there. I don't know what to do."

"You can close your account."

She wraps her arms around her stomach. Shakes her head in despair. "I can't believe this. It's more of the same. At school. On the bus. Out in public. I'm used to people staring. But the taunting. And now threats."

"Have you told anyone? Your parents? Someone at school?"

She shakes her head.

"Maybe you need to. You shouldn't have to feel scared and sick all the time."

She nods. Looks down at her laptop. "I don't want to do anything more on the computer. If that's okay with you."

"Sure. I understand. I'll go." I pull my feet up and try to get out of the beanbag chair.

"You don't have to leave," she says.

"Good. Because I can't."

She smiles and helps me up. "Would you like to stay for dinner?" she asks when I'm on my feet. "It will help keep my mind off of … that." She points at her computer.

"Are you sure?" I ask.

"Yes. It's fine. It would be nice."

Dinner would be awesome if I could stop worrying about Nasreen. I'm worried for myself too. I was included in one of those ugly comments.

And then there's the whole cultural thing about eating with a Muslim family. I don't know the rules, and I'm afraid of doing something offensive. But Nasreen's parents are really polite. They keep offering me food, which is delicious. Something with lentils. And there's this fantastic flat bread and rice and veggies. Her brother, Jaffar, is mostly quiet. He keeps glancing over at me. And when he does, his mom glances at *him*. I feel like *I* should be wearing a hijab and a wool coat.

Nasreen told me he's nineteen. She didn't tell me that he's, well, handsome. Thick black hair. Black eyebrows over deep-set, dark eyes. A nose that's kind of big but perfect for his face. A pouty bottom lip. But he's Nasreen's brother and Muslim and other things that I'm sure make him not eligible. Who knows, maybe he's been promised to some girl in an arranged marriage. So I try not to stare.

"Nasreen, what's wrong?" her mother asks midway through the meal. She has a heavy accent that's a little hard to understand. "You're very quiet. And you're hardly eating."

Nasreen raises her eyes and pastes on a smile. "Nothing's wrong. I'm fine." She pushes food around her plate with her fork.

"So what schools have you guys been looking at?" Jaffar asks. His voice sounds American, like Nasreen's.

"MIT, Stanford, and the University of Iowa so far," Nasreen says.

He rolls his eyes. "Now there's a combination."

"Is your father a professional?" Mr. Talpur asks.

I'm glad my mouth is full. It gives me a chance to think how to answer. "No," I say, keeping it short and sweet. "But his mom was a math teacher. I think I got my math brains from her."

"Mia just moved in with her grandmother," Nasreen explains.

"My mom's mom," I clarify.

"Ah, I see," Mrs. Talpur says.

The room is quiet. I can hear the unasked questions hanging in the air. Like, why am I living with my grandmother? Where's my mom? Where's my dad? Everything about my past is so complicated. I fidget. Feel like I should tell them something.

"My mom is … away," I finally say. "I'm not sure where my dad is. Gram is my closest relative. Well, the closest relative who had room for me." I don't add that she was the only relative willing to take me in. Or that the last time I saw her before this past weekend was fourteen years ago. When I was three and she and my mom had a big fight.

Now Jaffar is openly staring. Everyone's looking at me. I pile lentils onto my fork. "This is really good. What is it?"

They slowly start talking about Pakistani food. I feel like I can breathe again.

Nasreen

I'm grateful Mia has stayed for dinner. Without her as a distraction, Mom would be even more insistent about finding out what's wrong. And I need time to think. Those online messages have gotten to me in a way the bullying at school hasn't. The words are there for everyone to see. Everyone in the world—even my family, if they bother to look. The comments are so ugly. So hateful. How do I defend myself?

I feel dirty. Violated. Like I want to crawl into a hole and die.

As I try to eat a few mouthfuls of dinner, I think about deleting my account, like Mia suggested. I should. Definitely. I also think about telling my parents. I haven't wanted to bother them before now. What can they do? Mom barely speaks English. Both Mom and Dad hate dealing with officials of any kind. But maybe Mia was right. Maybe it's time. I'm so tired of feeling sick and frightened. Who knows, maybe my parents will surprise me.

The meal finished, I see Mia out and close the door.

My father is reading the newspaper in the living room. I sit on the couch next to him. "Dad?" I say, thinking about how I'm going to word this.

He lowers the paper and glances at my hijab. "I'm ashamed you have to cover your hair in the house."

I'm taken aback. "What?"

"We should live in a place where you can have Muslim friends. I'm sorry."

"Dad. It's not your fault."

"Yes, it is. We should have moved to a Pakistani community when I lost my job. I can be a gardener in Los Angeles as easily as here."

"It doesn't matter to me that Mia isn't Muslim. Or Pakistani."

"It matters to me."

"Are you saying I shouldn't be friends with her?"

He *harrumphs*. "I assume she's Christian. With a questionable background."

"So what if she's Christian? And how does her background matter?"

He raises the paper back up to his face without answering.

I can't talk to him. I jump up from the couch and stride into the kitchen.

"I was wondering where you were," Mom says, speaking Punjabi. "Help me with the dishes."

"What do you think of Mia?" I set dirty dishes on the counter.

She shrugs. "Seems nice enough. Bright."

I sigh. "Good. I'm glad you like her."

"I didn't say I liked her."

I roll my eyes. "Well, *I* like her." I drop a plate into the dishwasher. "That's all that should matter."

She doesn't say anything. I take a deep breath. "Mom, there's something I want to talk to you about."

She silently scrubs the rice pot.

"There's a group of girls at school," I say, trying to find the right words. "They're not very nice to me."

"What do you mean, *not nice*?"

"They call me names. They say bad things about me."

She shakes her head as she rinses the pot. "This never would have happened in Pakistan. Do you want to stop wearing your hijab?"

"No! I just...." I think about it. What do I want? "I just want it to stop."

"Ignore them," Mom says. "In a year and a half you'll be graduating." She hands me the pot.

"But I *have* been ignoring them." I dry the pot with a towel. "And it's not working."

"Are you doing something to cause them to dislike you?"

"No, of course not! I'm just being me."

She runs water in the sink. Her narrowed eyes and creased brow tell me the whole story. She's imagining going to school. She's imagining talking to the principal and trying to make herself understood. The idea fills her with dread. It's the last thing in the world she wants to do.

"Never mind," I tell her. "I'll take care of it."

She faces me and pats my cheek with her damp hand. "You are beautiful and brilliant. You are firm in your faith. These girls are just jealous."

"Yeah. Maybe." I step away from the sink and shove the pot in a drawer. Of course it's not that simple. But I'm not going to force my mother into a situation that frightens her. I know how that feels.

My parents *have* surprised me. Just not in the way I wanted.

I finish in the kitchen and return to my bedroom. I have a research paper I should be working on for government. Instead, I flip open my laptop. I tell myself I'm just going online to delete my Facebook account. But I can't help it. I read through the comments again, one by one. The words are still ugly and hateful. But the initial shock has worn off. I'm more analytical now. I make note of who sent each comment and when. I go to the senders' home pages.

Not surprisingly, the main culprits are Samantha, Melody, and Rachel. But there are others too. Kyle, the boy who sits behind me on the bus. He's responsible for a couple of the sexual messages.

There are a few names I don't recognize. These people seem to be from all over the place, not just Arondale High. I feel sick to my stomach again. How did this ever happen? How did it ever blow up like this?

I notice links to other social networking sites on Samantha's page. I click on one of the links. It's mostly photos. I scroll down and my heart stops. There's a photo of a young woman wearing a dark *niqab*, a head covering showing only the woman's eyes and the bridge of her nose. Around her is a red circle with a red-slanted line cutting through it. Across the image are the words "Boycott Muslims" and "Muslim Free Zone."

Beneath the photo are comments about Muslims in general, but also about me. How much I suck. How much they wish I wasn't at school.

I close my laptop, wishing I were dead.

CHAPTER 8

Mia

I walk the mile home from Nasreen's house thinking about the unfairness of things. Like how some kids get picked on and others don't. How Jaffar is off-limits. How religion separates people in such weird ways. Same with race and skin color. I feel judged even when it's not obvious. The side looks. The lack of eye contact. Nasreen's parents were being polite, but I know they were judging me. For being black as much as for not being Muslim.

I guess it's fair my mom is in prison. She did break the law, way more times than she ever got caught. But it's unfair her problems keep screwing up my life. It's definitely unfair my dad disappeared before I was born. I'm in such a snarky mood, even the neatly trimmed shrubs along Gram's block seem unfair. Who decides who gets to live in a nice neighborhood? Is it luck? The situation you're born into? Effort? Brains?

I hope it's effort and brains. Because as much as I miss my friend Delia, I don't want to go back to Chicago. Talk about mean girls. A punch to the kidneys when no one is looking. Full-on fistfights. Though in some ways, physical violence is easier to cope with than the underhanded crap going on at Arondale High. But after one week of school, I've decided I want to make this work. Whether it's fair or not, I'm getting a good education. At least kids aren't judging me for wanting to study and get good grades. And I like Nasreen.

I never imagined I'd make a friend so quickly.

I'll deal with the bullying.

I walk into the house. Gram is watching a cop show on TV. I think about taking my own advice. Talking to her. I sit on the couch.

"Hi, Mia. How was your outing?"

Outing? "Um, we didn't go out."

"Oh." A commercial comes on and she finally focuses on me. "I was wondering if we should visit your mother."

My throat closes up. "She's in Indiana."

"I know. We could drive there some weekend. Don't you want to see her?"

I stare at the commercial for floor cleaner. Visit my mom in prison? Why? So my heart can break all over again? "Let me think about it."

"Sure." The program comes back on. Gram is back to playing junior detective.

I get up and go to my room. She can't help me. She doesn't have a clue. About anything.

Monday morning I get to the bus stop. Kids seem more used to me now. At least no one stares. The bus arrives and I climb on. I'm relieved to see Nasreen in her usual spot. I had a bad feeling on Sunday. Like she told her parents what was happening and they decided to pull her out of school.

"Hi," I say.

She smiles but it doesn't quite reach her eyes.

Then I hear from the back, "You guys are so cute together!"

"How about a threesome?" a smarmy voice says right behind me.

My skin crawls. I glance over at Nasreen. She's staring at the top of her backpack, which she's hugging to her chest. I wonder if this has been going on since she got on the bus this morning.

"Come on," the kid behind me says. I think his name is Kyle. "You, me, and the Muslim. It'll be fun."

What is going on? Last week it wasn't so blatant. I'm not sure how to handle this. If I turn around and say something, it will just escalate. A fistfight on the bus could get nasty. So I sit there. Stare straight ahead. Trapped.

We get to school, and the bus jerks to a stop. I jump up. Just want out of here. But the driver is having trouble with the door or something. We're packed in the aisle. People are yelling. Jostling.

Behind me Nasreen screams, "STOP IT!"

The bus quiets. Then a bunch of kids laugh. I twist around, knowing it must be really bad for her to yell like that. She's facing Kyle. I glare at him over Nasreen's shoulder. He's got a slimy grin on his face that quickly fades when he sees me. He says, "What are you looking at, sista?"

Only he didn't say "sista." No. A couple kids gasp. My face burns. My hands are shaking. I'm pushing Nasreen out of the way. I'm going to slug him. I'm going to wipe that ugly smirk off his face.

"Hey! Get off the bus already!" It's someone behind Kyle. I turn around. The aisle is clear in front of me. I give Kyle one last glare. His expression is still smug, but his upper lip twitches. I hope that means I scared him. I hope he feels bad about what he said. I march down the aisle.

I jump down the steps. Nasreen is right next to me. "Don't fight him," she says, nudging me forward. "Don't turn around."

I can't believe Nasreen is giving me bullying advice. But she's right. If I fight, I'll get suspended. That's always the way it is. We walk quickly down the main hallway.

"This way," she says. She leads me out the back to an outdoor eating area. It's blissfully empty. She drops her backpack on a bench and rubs her arms. We're both breathing hard. She glances into my eyes, then looks down again. "I'm sorry he said that."

"Asshole," I say. Then I ask, "Why did you yell at him?"

"He …" She bites her bottom lip. Her eyes fill with tears. "He rubbed up against me. His … front."

I shake my head. What a friggin' scumbag. That's humiliating for anyone. But for Nasreen? I reach out and squeeze her arm. She cries openly. Sits on the bench. "I'm sorry for crying again," she says. "I'm so weak."

I sit next to her. "Did you talk to your parents this weekend?"

She nods but doesn't say anything. I have a feeling it didn't go well.

"What's the counselor here like?" I ask.

"He's okay. But I've never spoken to him about anything personal."

"Let's talk to him today, okay? Both of us. At lunch."

She takes a deep breath and wipes her eyes. Tries to smile. "Okay."

The bell rings. We get to our feet and head for first period.

"Why was the bus so bad this morning?" I ask.

"Substitute driver," she says. "They never write anyone up."

As we walk, I get the impression of a war zone. And Nasreen and I are right in the middle of it. This is *so* not what I expected of the suburbs.

CHAPTER 9

Nasreen

Like I do every day, I walk past the counselor's office between first and second period. Mr. Clarke's room is in a little hallway off the main corridor. It's not completely out in the open. But it's not really private either. You can look down there and see who's coming in or out. Who's waiting in the chairs.

At the moment, his door is ajar and the chairs are empty. I face forward and speed up. The idea of going in there worries me. Will his advice be the same as my mom's? That bullying is part of growing up. The girls are jealous. I'm doing something to cause it.

But what happened on the bus this morning was so disgusting. What's happening online is terrible. Mia is right. We have to tell an adult.

I have trouble focusing in my morning classes. I barely got all of my homework done over the weekend. I went online a few more times. I know I shouldn't have. It was stupid and made me feel awful. But I wanted to know what they were saying.

I sit next to Mia in calculus. We hardly say anything to each other. I'm starting to get nervous. Part of me hopes she's forgotten about seeing the counselor. But when the bell rings, she says, "Ready?"

I shrug.

"Come on. You have to show me where it is."

Even walking down the little hallway

makes my heart pound. The door is closed. There's a sign with a smiley face on it.

Back in a minute
Have a seat ☺

Mia flops onto one of the chairs against the wall. I look furtively toward the main hallway. It's packed with kids going to lunch or their next class. Some glance our way, curious, like I've done so many times. My heart thumps faster. "How long should we wait?" I ask.

"I don't know. As long as it takes, I guess. Do what the sign says, Nasreen. Have a seat."

"I can't." I stay standing, looking toward the hallway. I see Samantha. My breath catches. She stares straight ahead, not paying attention. I'm just about to start breathing again when Rachel looks at me. Oh no. She stops walking. Her jaw drops.

I can't hear what she says, but Melody and Samantha back up. Now they're all staring at us.

"Crap," Mia mutters. She sees them too.

They walk toward us. "Hi, girls," Samantha says in an overly sweet voice. She stops in front of me. I step back. My leg hits the empty chair.

"If you're thinking about chatting with Mr. Clarke about us, don't," she says. "You won't believe how much worse it'll get." She glares at Mia. Then she scowls at me before they turn and leave.

Mia gets to her feet. "Crap," she repeats.

I can't imagine Samantha's bullying getting any worse. Then I realize it can. Of course it can. "How is the counselor going to help us?" I ask.

Mia shrugs. "Don't know."

"I don't think I can do this."

She sighs. "Yeah. What's he going to do? Sit with us on the bus? Walk with us in the hallways?"

Both of us are quiet as we make our way to the lunchroom. I'm back to my original method of dealing with Samantha and Kyle—keeping my head down. It's not working very well, but I don't know what else to do.

"I brought my lunch today," Mia says.

"No pizza?"

"Nah. It's starting to taste like cardboard. And I'm feeling a little guilty for spending Gram's money."

We head to my favorite place, a low wall near the soccer field. It's nice having someone sit with me. She swings her legs, her heels pounding against the cement. I notice the rips in her jeans.

"Sometimes I wonder what it would be like to wear jeans," I say.

"I've noticed you only wear long

skirts," Mia says. "Is that part of the whole modesty thing?"

I nod. "So the curves of my body don't show."

Mia gazes out at the field. "I could use a wardrobe update. It might help me fit in with the whole suburban vibe. Not that I want to be suburban, but …" Her voice trails off.

"I understand," I say. "One less thing to feel different about."

Mia grins. "See? I love that about you. You totally get it."

I'm glad I get it. Glad she gets me. She could have teased me about wearing skirts, but she didn't. I get an idea. Before I change my mind, I ask, "Would you like to go shopping this weekend? I think my brother will drive us. If I ask him nicely."

"Sure," Mia says right way.

It's hard to believe I can still smile

after the morning we've had. "Do you have brothers or sisters?" I ask.

"Nope. Only me." She takes a bite of her sandwich.

"The other night you said your mother is away. I don't know what I'd do without my mother."

"Believe me, you'd survive." Mia wraps up the rest of her sandwich and shoves it in her backpack. "I'm going to the restroom. See you in study hall." She throws her backpack over her shoulder and strides away.

Our lives are very different. But as I watch Mia leave, it strikes me that one thing we have in common is our shoulders. We both slouch. I think it's because we're trying to protect our hearts.

CHAPTER 10

Mia

When Nasreen says something about my mom during lunch, I clam up. I trust her—probably more than I trust Delia. And I don't think she'd judge me. But it's embarrassing. "My mom's in prison." There's no way to say it that doesn't make my left eye twitch and my pits sweat. So I escape to the restroom, holding onto my secret. There are some things no one else needs to know.

Nasreen must have gotten the hint. She doesn't mention it again the rest of the week. Monday on the bus was definitely the worst. Thankfully, the regular driver came back on Tuesday. Kyle still said crap to us that the driver couldn't hear. But he didn't repeat *that* word. If he ever does, I swear I'm killing him.

Now it's Saturday. I'm waiting on the front porch for Nasreen and her brother to pick me up. A shopping trip to a suburban mall. Whoopee. Actually, I'm happy to be getting out of the house. Plus, I really do need something besides gray and black in my closet. And, best of all, I'll get to ogle Nasreen's brother.

A dark blue car pulls up. Nasreen waves from the passenger seat.

"Hey," I say, jumping into the back.

Jaffar nods at me in the rearview mirror. He holds my eyes a little longer than he needs to. My stomach flutters.

"Have you been to the fabulous Arondale Mall yet?" he asks.

"No."

"You are in for a real treat," he adds sarcastically.

"It's not that bad," Nasreen says.

"Yes, it is that bad. I don't know why I agreed to this." But I can tell by his reflection in the mirror that he's smiling.

The mall is huge. We're standing at a fountain. Water flows over cement rocks and down a miniature river. It is kind of amazing in a naturally fake way.

"Where to first?" Nasreen asks.

"My only requirement is cheap," I tell her. "My hundred bucks from Gram won't go far. Not if I'm paying full price."

Nasreen and Jaffar argue a little. I'm wondering why he's hanging out with us. Not that I'm sorry. But I figured he'd just drop us off or do his own mall thing.

We hit a couple of clothing stores. I find a violet hoodie on sale. A pair of jeans with no holes. At a third store, I consider a blouse like ones I've seen girls wear at school. Decide against it. I have to be true to my style. I grab two solid-colored

T-shirts. Nasreen picks out a couple of loose-fitting tops. Like at the other stores, Jaffar waits outside, pacing.

"What's with your brother?" I ask while we're in line to pay. "Why is he waiting for us?"

She bites her bottom lip. Says softly, "He's my escort."

"Your what?" Her cheeks turn red. I quickly figure it out. "Oh, it's a religious thing. Sorry."

"That's okay. My parents don't insist on it. I mean, I go to school on my own. But I feel more comfortable …" Her voice trails off. Then she says, "It was my idea. I asked him."

"Oh," is all I can think to say. "Man, this line is taking forever." I want to change the subject instead of saying what's really on my mind. *A flippin' escort? You're that scared?* But then I think of Kyle behind her on the bus. All the comments and stares she gets, even here at the mall.

"Someone's making a return," Nasreen says, peering around the customer in front of us. She smiles slyly. "Jaffar was strangely happy to come, by the way. I think that has something to do with you."

Okay, this is embarrassing. I take a deep breath. Rearrange the shirts over my arm.

"Don't worry, I won't tell my parents."

"They'd kill him, wouldn't they?"

She laughs. "Oh, definitely. They'd kill you too." My eyes must have gone wide. "I'm just kidding," she adds quickly. "They'd only maim you."

I'm glad she's still laughing.

The line finally moves. We pay and leave the store with our bags.

"I hope that's it," Jaffar says when we meet him outside the store. "I'm starving."

"Has to be it," I tell him. "I'm down to five bucks."

"Food court!" Nasreen shouts. She trots down the hallway, swinging her shopping bags. When she turns to us, her grin spreads from ear to ear. "Hurry up!"

I've only known Nasreen a couple of weeks. But something tells me this good mood is a rarity for her. It is for me too. The smile on my face is real. Even on my best days in Chicago, I had a constant weight on my shoulders. Life with Mom was one big stress bucket. And I'm beginning to realize my friendship with Delia didn't help. She was always trying to talk me into doing crazy stuff. Like that picture of her jumping off the car? Typical Delia. She didn't care about school or studying. Just messing around.

"Get what you wanted?" Jaffar asks me.

"I think so." I notice Nasreen is still walking ahead of us. I wonder if she's leaving us alone on purpose.

"How are you liking Arondale?" His gorgeous smile sends my stomach fluttering again.

"It's … okay."

"Yeah. Hard to fit in. I'm still not used to it."

"Will you move back to Pakistan when you finish college?" I ask.

"I don't know. I visited once. But I've lived in America all my life. Pakistan didn't exactly feel like home."

"Sounds like you're confused."

"Totally." He smiles again. Holds my eyes a few seconds too long, like he did in the car.

I glance away, feeling self-conscious. The food court is coming up.

He slows his pace. Lets Nasreen get farther ahead of us. "I know this is a strange question," he says softly. "But are you Christian?"

Wow. Okay. That *is* an odd question.

"Um, not exactly," I say. "I mean, historically. But I'm not practicing."

He nods. Looks relieved and disappointed at the same time.

"Why?" I ask.

"This is totally wrong. I shouldn't even ask. But if you're not über-Christian, I at least have some hope that you might go out with me."

I laugh. "Is this your way of asking me on a date?"

"Yes. Next Saturday. Movie and fast-food restaurant of your choice."

I shrug. "Okay. Sure."

Nasreen has stopped walking. She squints as she waits for us. "What are you guys whispering about?"

"None of your business," Jaffar says.

I take a deep breath. Actually, it is her business. I hope she doesn't mind if I date her brother. I like my friendship with her too much to ruin it.

CHAPTER 11

Nasreen

After shopping, Jaffar and I drop Mia off at her house. I had a great time. Yes, people stared. Yes, they gawked at my hijab. But for once I didn't care. I felt strangely normal. Like how I imagine I'd feel walking down a street in Pakistan. Just another young woman out with her friend.

Jaffar pulls away from the curb. He turns up the car radio.

I turn it down.

"Hey," he complains.

"I have a question," I say. "Do you think two weeks is long enough to know if someone is a good friend? Like, a best friend?"

"I don't know." He turns the volume back up.

I sigh and turn it back down. "Please answer me."

He sighs. "Only you can answer that question. Do you think Mia is a good friend?"

I think about it. I really like her. I trust her. She seems uncomfortable talking to me about her past, so I'm not sure that she trusts *me*. But she does seem to like me. "Yes. I guess I do."

Jaffar shrugs. "There you go."

I stare at my brother. "Did you ask her out?"

His jaw tenses.

"I hope you know what you're doing," I say.

He sighs. "Yeah, me too. You won't tell Mom and Dad, will you?"

"No, of course not. But what if it gets serious? They'll find out."

"It's just a date, okay? One date."

"Right." I turn the radio volume up for him.

Jaffar is not as devout as the rest of our family. But I never thought he'd date a girl who wasn't Muslim. I'm not sure how I feel about it. Since I like Mia, it's hard to not be happy for them. I just hope she doesn't fall too hard for him. Jaffar can be impulsive. I wonder if he's really thought this through.

That normal feeling lasts all weekend and into Monday. I feel … different. Samantha yells something stupid when I get on the bus. I don't shrink into my seat. I don't lower my chin to my chest. It feels good not to be so mousy. The stop after mine, Kyle gets on. I try to keep my shoulders squared as I steel myself for his morning slurs.

But instead of sitting behind me, he slides in next to me.

My skin prickles. I don't want him so close. I open my mouth to say something. Then I close it. I build up my courage again. "This seat is saved," I murmur.

"What was that?" he asks.

"I said this seat is saved!"

"I'm sorry, I still didn't hear you."

Of course he heard me. Everyone around us did. I don't know what to do. Arguing won't make him leave. But I don't want to shrink into myself either. I felt too good a second ago to go back to the way I was. "Whatever," I say, recognizing Mia's sarcasm in my voice.

He snickers. "Your scarf is ravishing this morning. That shade of blue makes me *want* you."

I can't stand this. If he won't leave, I will.

I look over my shoulder. The seat

behind me is still completely empty. When the bus stops at Mia's corner, I wait until she's approaching down the aisle. Then I jump up and step over Kyle's feet. He raises his leg. I trip and fall across the aisle.

Kyle laughs hysterically. So do his friends.

The girl I've fallen into pushes me away. "Get off!"

Mia helps me up. "You okay?" she asks.

"Yes," I answer. But I'm not okay. I'm humiliated. I'm angry. Like I always am on this stupid bus. I turn to Kyle. I'm shaking. My cheeks are burning. "Asshole!" I hiss into his face.

I hear more laughter, including Kyle's. "What did you just say?"

The driver must have noticed the commotion. "What's going on over there?" she says, twisting in her seat.

"She's calling me bad names!" Kyle whines.

The driver glares at us. "Cool it. Or I'll write you both up."

The bus door closes. By now, there are no empty seats. Mia and I have to sit with other people. My heart is beating like a rabbit's. I can barely catch my breath. I can't believe I said that to Kyle. What was I thinking?

I feel a hand on my shoulder. I tense up. But then I hear Mia whisper, "That was awesome."

I nod. But if it was so awesome, why am I trembling? At least I'm not sitting next to Kyle, taking his verbal abuse. He keeps turning and staring. Puckering his lips. I look out the window and force myself to breathe.

My heart is still skipping when we walk into school. I can't seem to take deep-enough breaths.

"Are you sure you're okay?" Mia asks.

"I don't know."

"Is that the first time you ever stood up for yourself?"

I nod.

She grins.

"What?" I ask.

"Like I said, that was awesome."

"But now what? He'll retaliate. It will get worse."

She seems to consider this. Shrugs. "At least you said something. That must have felt a *little* good."

She's right. It did feel a little good. I give her a small smile.

We separate and go to our first-period classes.

It's not until the middle of first period that my pulse and breathing slow back to normal. But I'm having a hard time focusing on chemistry. I keep thinking about how I've been treated at school. All of the

harsh words I've tried to ignore. The trip-
ping, the thrown pencils, the shoves. The
parties and dances I've never been invited
to. The problem is, I haven't really ignored
any of it. It's all sunk in. When I yelled
at Kyle on the bus, there were a hundred
other vicious things I wanted to say.

It feels like my anger is a shaken soda
pop, ready to explode. Saying that one
word, it's like I barely twisted the cap
open. A little fizzed away. But there's so
much more pressure in the bottle. The
depth of my anger scares me. I rub my
temples, fighting a headache.

Mia

Monday on the bus is pure hell. Watching Nasreen stand up for herself against Kyle is cool, but I can tell it shakes her up. She seems a little different. A little more confident.

On Wednesday, Samantha and her buddies walk up behind us on our way to lunch.

"Hey, sweethearts." I recognize Melody's voice. One of them makes kissing sounds.

I take a deep breath. Fine. Whatever.

Then Melody says, "You two must like dark meat."

"That's good," says Samantha. "Leaves the good white meat for the rest of us."

I stop walking and brace my feet against the floor. One of them runs into me. "Oops, sorry," I say as Melody staggers and almost falls. "Guess I wanted a little of that white meat to rub off on me."

"Bitch," Melody says, righting herself.

"Oh my," I say. "Watch the language, girl."

The three of them glare. They step around us. I figure the incident is over. We can carry on with our lives. But as they're walking to the lunchroom, Nasreen yells after them, "*You're* the bitches! Leave us alone!"

What had been a semi-private incident is suddenly public. People in the packed hallway gawk. Some stop to see what will happen next. Samantha, Rachel, and Melody turn as one. Samantha stares at Nasreen like a space alien just landed outside the lunchroom. My fingers twitch. At my old school, this is when a fight would start. Samantha looks from Nasreen to me. Her hands ball into fists. So do mine.

Melody nudges Samantha's arm. Samantha looks past us and her jaw slackens. I know that look. Someone in authority is nearby. Samantha gives Nasreen the evil eye and casually flips her off. Then they turn and stride into the lunchroom.

"Bitches," Nasreen mutters as we make our way outside.

I stare at her. I'm admiring this new Nasreen, but in the span of a few days, she's flipped from meek to macho. It feels a little crazy. "What brought that on?" I ask.

Matter-of-factly she says, "They're bitches."

"Well, yeah." We've reached our lunch spot. I jump up on the wall and unwrap my peanut butter sandwich. "But how does pissing them off get them to leave you alone?"

She sits on the wall next to me. Stares at the lunch bag on her lap. "I don't know. How do you do it?"

"Humor and sarcasm. It takes practice." Then I feel bad for ruining her fierce mood. "Don't worry about it, Nasreen." I take a bite of my sandwich. "So tell me about your brother," I say, wanting to get her mind on other things. "Quirks. Stupid habits." I told her on Monday that he'd asked me out. Thankfully, she already knew. And she seems okay with it.

"Well. …" She gazes into the distance. "He plays his music too loud. I'm sure he's ruining his hearing."

"Okay. So if I whisper, he may not hear me."

"He's smart," she continues. "But he doesn't think he is. He's kind of sensitive about it."

"Fine. No solving calculus equations on our first date."

She glances at me before opening her lunch bag.

"What?"

"I worry for you," Nasreen says. "You seem to really like him. And he's Muslim."

"Duh, I'm aware of this. If it's such a big deal, why did he ask me out in the first place?"

She digs her fork into her plastic container. "Because he likes you too. If my parents find out, they'll be totally against it. They want him to marry a Muslim."

"Marry!" I almost spit out a wad of peanut butter. "We're going for a burger and a movie. Is that like a marriage proposal in Pakistan?"

She smiles. Shakes her head. "Just be careful with your heart."

"Oh, I will. I'm an expert at that." I shove the last bite in my mouth. It's too big, and I have to chew it with my mouth open.

Nasreen gives me a side-glance.

"Sorry," I say. "I'm being gross."

"It's not that. I'm curious about your heart. How it's been broken."

My mom, I think. *Because she made too many promises she couldn't keep.* But I still don't want to talk about her. I pull an apple out of my bag. Twist off the stem. "Just … life."

For a while, the only sound is our chewing. Then Nasreen says, "Life. Life is a bitch."

I laugh. "You are totally fixated on that word today."

She laughs with me. Then she says quietly, "Sometimes I feel like I might explode. I used to just be scared of those kids. Now I'm also angry. I mean *really* angry."

"Like in the hallway before lunch?"

"Yes. I know I didn't handle that well. But I couldn't stop myself." She looks at me. "You seem to have it all figured out. How do you stay so calm?"

I shrug. "I'm not calm. It's all an act. On the inside I want to tear their heads off." Then I say, "I think it's cool you're not so scared anymore."

"I'm still scared," she says. "I think that's the problem. But I'm sick of my fear."

CHAPTER 13

Nasreen

It ends up being one of my best weeks at Arondale High School. After the incident outside the lunchroom, Samantha and her friends don't bother us. No one laughs or throws anything at me in any of my classes. Even Kyle leaves me alone. I wonder if it's because I've been standing up for myself. It doesn't matter. I'm just relieved. And I'm grateful to Mia. Her confidence is rubbing off on me. Just having a friend is making me feel better about myself.

Friday night I'm sitting in my beanbag

chair. I'm bored with the English essay I'm writing. I save the file and tap my fingers on the keyboard. My phone buzzes with a text. Family members and Mia are the only people who ever text me. I have a feeling it's Jaffar, too lazy to walk to my room and ask a favor. Maybe he wants me to iron a shirt for his big date tomorrow. "No way," I mutter to myself, grabbing the phone.

But the text is from a name I don't recognize—*Fidodish*. How did this person get my number? There's an Internet link with the message:

You might want to see this.

I go online and type in the address. On the top of the page is the title *Ugliest Girls at Arondale High*. It's a poll. At the top of the list is my name. Under my name is Mia's. There are lots of votes—over a hundred. And many comments, similar to the ones I'd seen online before:

Super skanky!
Might be something worthwhile under that scarf. Totally doubt it! ;)
Send the darkies back where they came from.

My hand is shaking as I scroll down the screen. I can't believe what I'm reading. My stomach churns. I thought things were getting better. They aren't. The bullying has just gone underground. Faceless. Nameless. This is so unfair. So disgusting! I want to crawl under my bed and never come out.

I think about telling someone, maybe Jaffar. But I'm too embarrassed. I don't want anyone in my family to know about this. I think about keeping it from Mia too. Why should both of us be miserable? But she has a right to know. It's not just about me, it involves her too. I send her a text forwarding the website link.

She calls me a minute later. "I got the same text you did," she says. "I'm looking at the poll now. What a pile of crap."

"What should we do?" My voice is shaking.

"Nothing. Pretend it doesn't exist."

"But it *does* exist."

"Not in my reality. I just backed out of that site. I'm never looking at it again."

"But—"

"Nasreen!" Mia snaps. "You have a choice. You can ignore it. You can do something about it, like tell the police or your parents. Or you can let the stress eat you up. That's exactly what these trolls want."

I don't know what to say.

"Are you closing that stupid screen?" Mia asks.

I hesitate. "Yes."

"Good. Now what are you going to do?"

"I'm going to forget about it," I whisper.

"Okay." Mia's voice softens. "I'm sorry for being tough on you. I know it's hard. But they're idiots. You know that, right?"

"Y … yes."

Mia sighs. "Guess I'd better go. I have to get my beauty sleep for my big date tomorrow."

"Okay," I respond.

"Are you all right, Nasreen? You sound kind of … crushed."

"I'm fine. See you Monday." I end the call.

I set my phone on the floor. I'm not really fine. Or confident. I don't close the site like I told Mia. I stare at the screen, like the words are being tattooed onto my eyes.

I had a hard time going to sleep that night. Who started that poll? Who's seen it? Everyone at school? What am I going to face on Monday? More insults? More laughter? More rejection?

I wake up late on Saturday morning with the same churning stomach. The same sense of humiliation. I don't know how to forget what I saw online. It's impossible.

Out in the hallway, Jaffar yells, "It's just a date!" His door slams.

Oh no. My parents must have found out about his date with Mia.

I hear a knock on his door. "Jaffar!" my dad says. "Jaffar!"

Jaffar turns up his music. The base thumps loudly through our shared wall. This is not good. Jaffar is being totally disrespectful. It's his fight, and I shouldn't get involved. But this is also about Mia, my friend. I want to defend her. Jumping out of bed, I throw on my robe. I open my door.

Dad is still standing in the middle of the hallway. His arms are crossed. He glares at me. "Did you know about this? That he's dating a Christian? That black girl?"

"That black girl is my friend. Her name is Mia."

He presses his lips together. His face is red. "This is completely unacceptable."

"Why didn't you tell us?" Mom asks. She's standing at the other end of the hallway wiping her hands on a kitchen towel. She's staring right into my eyes.

"Why should I? It's Jaffar's date, not mine. And they seem to like each other."

This is the wrong thing to say. I regret it the second it's out of my mouth. Mom and Dad exchange a look. I can tell they're imagining a Christian wedding. Non-Muslim grandkids they'll never see. Dad

shakes his head. He steps down the hallway toward Mom. They whisper as they
make their way to the kitchen.

The music is still really loud. I knock
anyway. "Jaffar!" I knock harder.

The door opens. He turns down his
music. He's pacing across the floor. His
room is so small, it only takes him a few
steps to get from one side to the other.

"How did they find out?" I ask, closing
the door behind me.

"I told Mom I wouldn't be here for
dinner. It kind of snowballed from there."
He runs his fingers through his hair. "I'm
nineteen. I should be able to see who I
want."

"It's not that simple," I say.

He stops walking and sighs. I know
he agrees with me. It's ingrained in us to
respect our parents. To respect our religion. Our heritage.

"What are you going to do?" I ask.

He's quiet a minute. Then he says, "I'm going out with Mia as planned."

I nod and go back to my room. I wonder if I should text Mia. Let her know what's going on. But I don't. This is between the two of them. I need to respect that she can handle this herself.

Mia

Am I happy? Yeah. I'm stoked. I thought about Jaffar all week. Honestly, I've been cloud-walking since he asked me out. When Samantha and her buds teased us on Wednesday, I didn't care. I didn't even care when I saw that stupid online poll last night. Because I knew today I was going out with a totally hot guy.

I wouldn't have met Jaffar without Nasreen. Even so, my only regret is that he and Nasreen are related. I can't exactly share my goofy feelings for him with his sister. So I've been playing it cool with Nasreen. Like tonight's date is no big deal.

It's a few minutes before he's supposed to pick me up. The butterflies in my stomach are having babies. I'm sitting in the living room with Gram watching TV news. I hear a car door slam. Jump up from the couch.

Gram snickers. "You're so antsy, Mia."

I walk to the window. Pull back the lace curtain. The neighbor across the street is backing his pickup truck out of his driveway. I wander to the hall mirror. Make sure I don't have lip gloss on my teeth.

"What's his name again?" Gram asks.

"Jaffar."

"What nationality is that?"

"Pakistani."

"He's from the Middle East?" she says, sounding slightly shocked.

I roll my eyes. "He's not a terrorist, Gram."

There's a knock at the door. My heart

thwacks in my chest. I force myself to take a couple of deep breaths before I open it. "Hey," I say. "Come in."

"Hey." He steps inside.

"Gram, this is Jaffar. Jaffar, this is my grandmother."

He steps into the living room and shakes her hand. "Hi," he says. "Nice to meet you."

Gram squints up at him. She's not smiling. "When will you have her home?"

He looks at me. Shrugs. "I don't know. Eleven?" I notice him glance at a pair of ceramic crosses above the fireplace.

"Okay, eleven," she says. "No later."

"Bye, Gram." I tug on Jaffar's sleeve, wanting to get out of here.

He opens the car door for me, but he isn't smiling. Doesn't say anything as he starts the engine. Doesn't even talk as he pulls away from the curb. It's not a comfortable silence. More like an extension of the awkwardness in the house. After a few blocks, I ask, "Everything okay?"

I expect him to smile. Say, "Sure. Everything's great."

Instead, he shakes his head. "No." He turns on to a side street. Parks the car in front of someone's house and turns off the engine. Twisting in his seat, he looks me in the eyes. "I can't do this."

"You can't do what? Drive?"

"No. I am very, very sorry. But I can't go out with you."

My heart stops. "Was it the crosses on the mantle? They're not mine. I told you, I'm not all that Christian."

"No, it wasn't the crosses. Well … partly the crosses." He closes his eyes and pounds his fist against his forehead. When he looks at me again, his eyes are so soft and beautiful I could melt.

"I like you, Mia," he says. "But you're not Muslim. That's a problem."

"A problem for who?"

"For my family. For your family. I could tell your grandmother didn't approve of me. Doesn't that mean anything to you?"

I shrug. "She's my guardian. If she doesn't like your religion or ethnicity, that's her problem."

He sighs. Looks out the windshield. "You're much stronger than I am."

"It's not strength. Family just isn't as important to me as it is to you." I think about my mom. All the different guys she's been with. He could be from Planet Xerox and worship copy paper and she wouldn't care. As long as he shared his cash.

I ask, "Are all of your dates this complicated?"

He taps the steering wheel. "That's the thing. I don't date much. Not many Muslim girls to choose from. And the ones I've found I'm not attracted to."

His roundabout way of saying he's attracted to me sends my stomach fluttering again. "So … why not follow your heart?"

His eyes are soft again when he looks at me. I'm beginning to hate that he's so gorgeous. I can see my heart is about to be broken.

"I'd like to," he says. "But as much as I think I can deny it, my religion is important to me. One of the most important things in my life."

"Yeah. Obviously." I close my eyes and take a deep breath. I'm a little jealous. Wish there was something I felt that strongly about. "I guess you'd better take me home."

"I'm sorry, Mia. I was looking forward to seeing you all week."

I expect him to start the car. Instead, I hear him tapping the steering wheel again. When I open my eyes, he's staring at me.

"What?" I ask.

"There is one thing." He takes a deep breath. "I don't know how to word this. You may hate me." He bites his bottom lip. "Would you ever consider changing religions?"

"You mean, become a Muslim?"

He nods and winces, like he's afraid I'll yell at him.

"Uh … wow. That's a huge question."

"I know," he says. "Sorry. Forget I asked, okay? Please?" He holds his palms together.

"Sure."

"Thank you." He shakes his head. "I'm such an idiot." He reaches for the ignition. Starts the car.

Neither of us says anything as he drives me back to Gram's house. My emotions are fighting over which is strongest. Anger that he got my hopes up. Disappointment that he's taking me home.

Sadness that a potential relationship never got a chance. I suppose I should feel insulted by his question. I guess I am. But I'm also a little flattered. He took a huge risk in asking. He wouldn't have bothered if he didn't care.

He pulls up in front of the house. At least Gram will be thrilled I'm not dating an infidel. I push the car door open.

"I would apologize again," Jaffar says. "But I'm already feeling incredibly lame." He sighs. "I will anyway. I'm sorry, Mia."

"Yeah. Me too." I look at him. "Would I have to wear a headscarf, like Nasreen?"

"What?" Then he gets what I'm asking. "Oh. It's a personal choice."

I nod and get out of the car. I don't look back. I'm curious what he's thinking. I'm curious what *I'm* thinking.

Nasreen

I feel miserable all Saturday. Mia was so confident about ignoring that online poll. She made it sound simple. But it's all I can think about. I obsessively watch it, keeping track of new comments, new votes. Mia and I are still at the top of the list. Last week, I thought the bullying was getting better. Now this.

It sends me tumbling.

I get sick of staring at the poll, sick of tormenting myself. I close my computer and go to the living room. I watch TV with my parents. We look up in surprise when

Jaffar walks in. He left for his date less than an hour ago.

"I'm not going out with Mia," he announces loudly, passing through the living room. "I hope you're all happy." He disappears down the hallway and slams his door.

I look at my parents. I expect them to be smiling. But the glances they exchange are sad. Knowing. I jump to my feet and go to Jaffar's room. I knock on his door and call his name a few times. He doesn't answer, just plays his music. I'm walking back to the living room when he opens his door a crack. "You were right," he says. "I should have listened to you."

"What happened?"

He closes his door without answering me.

I try to remember what I told him. I think I said dating who he wanted wasn't that simple. He must have decided against dating a non-Muslim. Poor Jaffar.

Poor Mia!

I go to my room and text her.

> You ok?

A minute later I get back:

> No. I need to borrow Koran.

What? That doesn't make sense. I text:

> Ok. I'll bring Monday. But ... ?????

She doesn't respond. I think of asking Jaffar if he knows what Mia wants with the Islamic holy book. But he's in such a foul mood, I decide against it. He stays shut in his room—and in his head—the rest of the weekend. He doesn't talk to any of us.

Getting myself to the bus stop Monday morning takes a huge effort. I feel myself reverting back to my old pattern. Hanging back. Eyes lowered. Shoulders hunched. I hate this lack of confidence. But I'm terrified—expecting the worst. I want to make myself small. Invisible.

As I sit in my usual seat, Samantha chants, "You're number one! You're number one!" Melody and Rachel join in. So do a few others. I know they're referring to the poll. And now I also know that a lot of kids have seen it.

"Okay," the driver grumbles. "Quiet down."

The chanting stops but everyone laughs. I shrink into my seat.

At the next stop, Kyle sits behind me. "Hi, Nasty. Did you see the list? It's totally bogus. *I* think you're very pretty."

My skin crawls.

I'm relieved at the next stop when Mia sits next to me. Having a friend makes me feel stronger. Like I'm not in this alone. But when she says, "Hey," I can barely hear her. She sounds as miserable and as weak as I feel.

I open my backpack and give her my Koran.

She takes it. Holds it a second. Hands it back to me. "I think I've changed my mind."

"Why did you want it in the first place?"

"Something Jaffar said."

"Wait," I say, guessing at the reason. "Did he suggest you convert to Islam?"

Mia shrugs. "Kind of."

I shake my head. "He shouldn't have done that."

"That's okay. I think he meant well."

As I raise the Koran to return it to my backpack, someone snatches it out of my hand. Behind me, Kyle holds it in the air, out of my reach.

My heart flies to my throat. "Give that back!" I yell, trying to grab it.

"Why?" he says. "Maybe I'd like to read it." He squints at the cover. "*The Holy Koran*." His eyes widen. "Is this your bible?"

"Yes. And I'd like it back!" Seeing him with the Koran my grandmother gave me makes me sick.

"Why? Am I not good enough for your stupid religion? What garbage." He shoves the book between his legs. Opens the window and picks up the book.

He's going to throw it out the window! I can't believe this. "No!" I shout.

Suddenly, Mia is leaning over the back of our seat. She grabs Kyle's wrist and hisses, "Let! Go!"

"*You* let go, bitch!" Kyle yells.

She yanks his wrist back. Hard. But he's still holding the book, reaching for the window. There's an uproar as kids around us yell. Laugh. Urge him to toss it.

The bus comes to an abrupt halt. The

driver trots down the aisle. "Stop it!" she bellows. "Both of you!"

Slowly, Mia and Kyle stop struggling. Before letting him go, Mia yanks the book out of his hand. She returns it to me.

The driver glares at them. "You two. When we get to school, stay on the bus." There are lots of "Oohs" and laughter from the other riders as the driver returns to her seat. I gently place the Koran in my backpack. Over our shoulders, Kyle mutters, "Butt-ugly sluts."

The driver escorts Mia and Kyle to the principal's office. All morning I hear classmates snickering. They make comments about the poll. Every student at school must know about it by now. My cheeks are constantly burning. I ignore everyone the best I can, but it's hard. I'd like to lock myself in a restroom stall the rest of the day.

I don't see Mia until third period. She walks into calculus late, frowning. She sinks into her seat. I hope she'll tell me what happened in the principal's office. But she doesn't say a word. When class ends, I ask, "Coming to lunch?"

She hesitates. "Yeah."

As we're walking down the main hall-way, Samantha calls, "Hey, it's the Arondale ugly—"

The word she calls us is so ugly, I expect Mia to go ballistic, the way she did on the bus. But she stares straight ahead. She picks up her pace.

We sit on our wall. I think we'll finally talk about what's going on. But she silently holds her unopened lunch bag on her lap. I look over, about to ask if she's okay.

But, clearly, she's not. Tears are running down her cheeks.

It's a horrible sight. A few days ago, Mia was so happy. So confident. I suddenly realize how much I look up to her. It jolts me to see her this wretched.

Then I feel angry. I'm angry at what's going on. I'm angry at what Mia and I are putting up with. It's got to stop. I don't care how it happens.

It has got to stop.

CHAPTER 16

Mia

On Saturday I'm walking from Jaffar's car into Gram's house. I'm thinking about how lousy I felt when I first got to Arondale. Then I met Nasreen and things started going good. Now I'm on the edge of a huge crap pile, about to fall in. I'm so determined to keep the crap at bay, I consider what Jaffar asked. I think about converting to Islam.

"You just left," Gram says when I walk into the living room. She's sitting in front of the TV, the same place I left her.

"Yeah. Something came up. Jaffar had to cancel."

"Everything okay?" she asks.

"Yeah. Fine. I'm gonna do some homework."

"By the way, have you thought about when you want to visit your mom?"

"No."

Once in my room, I flip open my laptop. Google Islam. I want to know what it's like to be Muslim. What they believe in. From what I read online, the basics are like a lot of religions. They believe in God. They have a main prophet, in this case Mohammed. They have a holy book, in this case the Koran. I'm just thinking I should read it when I get a text from Nasreen. She wants to know if I'm okay. I don't want to describe my date fail. But I do ask if I can borrow a Koran.

All day Sunday, I think about converting. What I conclude is that I don't think this is how it's supposed to work. Converting to a religion to impress a guy isn't right. And it all comes crashing. I was so high on Jaffar. On having him as a boyfriend. But it's not going to happen. I slide deep into the crap pile. Feel worse than I did the day I arrived in Arondale. Like a nothing. Like a nobody. And suddenly that online poll about the ugliest girls at Arondale High hits home. It kicks me in the gut. I feel ugly, so maybe it's true.

It doesn't totally surprise me on Monday when I get into a fight on the bus. That's what I do when I'm feeling like a nothing. Because I don't have anything to lose. Plus, Kyle is such a jerk, he deserves to get his ass kicked. But there are always consequences to fighting. I know this. So it's also no surprise when the bus driver marches Kyle and me into the school office.

We sit a couple of chairs apart. Both of us have our arms crossed. I stare at my feet. I feel him glaring at me, daggers shooting out of his eyes. Like he's daring me to get him into trouble. And now I'm thinking maybe talking to the principal isn't such a bad thing. Maybe it's a chance to finally explain the hell Nasreen and I go through every morning and afternoon.

The driver leaves Principal Willems's office. He steps into the waiting area and sighs loudly. "Come in, both of you." He sits at his desk. "You were fighting over a book?"

"It was a Koran," I say, wanting to get my side in first. "He was about to throw it out the window."

"Liar!" Kyle says. "I'd just opened the window for some air. I asked the headscarf girl if I could see her book."

I gape at him. "Her name is Nasreen!" I feel like twisting his arm again. "And you didn't ask for the book. You grabbed it out of her hand."

"I did not," he whines.

"Okay, okay," Willems says.

I cross my arms and slouch. "We sit through his crap every bus ride. He makes sexual comments—"

Kyle grunts. "Right."

"He called me *that* word!"

Kyle rolls his eyes and shakes his head.

"Did you call her that?" Willems asks.

"Of course not."

The principal nods. That's when I realize they're on the same page. They're in the same club. Kyle's the insider. I'm the outsider. Nothing is going to happen. Nothing is going to change. "He's a goddamn bully!" I shout.

"Hey!" Willems glares at me. "That language may be acceptable in the city, but not here." He gets to his feet. "I'm not going to suspend either of you. But you're on warning." His eyes stay glued on me longer than on Kyle.

I turn and march out of his office.

I hardly talk to Nasreen in calculus. Which isn't fair. None of this is her fault. Samantha and her sidekicks toss us a few choice insults as we walk to lunch. I don't respond. It's like I've forgotten how. Their jibes just pound me farther into the crap pile.

We reach our eating spot. As I sit on the wall, I can't remember ever feeling so worthless. I don't even have the courage to see my mom in jail. For all her faults, she always tried to take care of me. She loves me. I know she's thinking about me. But I can't see her in there. I just can't.

The tears come. I let them.

Nasreen does the right thing. She doesn't ask me a bunch of questions. She just sits quietly.

When I'm finally cried out, I take a deep breath. "Thanks," I say.

"For what?" she says.

"For being a good friend."

She nods. "Let me know if you ever want to talk about it."

Before last period, I stop at my locker. A folded piece of paper falls out when I open the door. I unfold it. It's a computer printout containing two sentences:

Bitch. I hate you. I'm going to kill you.

My hand starts shaking. I hear a rushing sound in my ears. I don't know how long I stand there, staring at those nine words. It's got to be a joke. I turn, glance up and down the hallway. No one is watching me, laughing or otherwise.

If I don't get to class now, I'll be late. I don't care. Slamming my locker closed, I carry the note and my backpack to the office. "I need to talk to the principal," I tell the secretary.

"I'm sorry, dear. He's unavailable."

I hear laughter and Willems's voice

filter out of his office. I look at the secretary. "I *have* to see him. It's urgent."

She sighs. Leaves. A minute later Principal Willems is standing across the counter from me. "What's the emergency?" He wipes a napkin across his mouth.

I toss the note on the counter. "I just found that in my locker."

He picks it up and reads it. His eyes widen. "Do you know who wrote this?"

"No. But a few people come to mind."

"Well … " He looks from the note to me. "I can see why you're upset. This is certainly not funny. But without knowing who put it in your locker, I'm not sure what I can do."

"You can start by questioning Kyle."

His eyes narrow. "You're really angry with him, aren't you?"

I stare at him in disbelief. "Yes! He's a liar. A bully."

Willems shakes his head. "I just don't

understand where this is coming from, Mia. Kyle is a model student. He's very popular."

My shoulders sag as reality sinks in again. I won't get any justice here. Slowly I take it from him. "Thanks. Whatever," I mutter.

"If you receive any more threats, let me know," the principal says as he turns to leave.

"Yeah," I say. "I'll do that."

CHAPTER 17

Nasreen

Study hall has already started when Mia hands a pass to Mrs. Belcher. Mia's face is scrunched up in a way I haven't seen before. Like she's depressed, angry, and scared all at the same time. She tosses a piece of paper on my desk. I unfold it. The words take my breath away. It's a threat. Someone's threatening to kill her? "Who gave this to you?" I ask.

She shrugs. "It was in my locker." She takes the note back from me.

My stomach tumbles. "What are you going to do?"

"Girls!" Mrs. Belcher says. "Quiet."

I look back at my history textbook, but I can't concentrate. Mia takes out her calculus homework. I doubt she's thinking about schoolwork either.

I have so many questions. At lunch she seemed to like that I kept my questions to myself. But I can't stand not knowing what's going on. And I want to tell her what I've been thinking about all day. Something I'm planning. Something that will set things right.

Class finally ends. As I'm gathering my books, I ask, "Do you want to come to my house?"

She hesitates. "I don't think that's such a good idea."

I wonder why. Then I realize she doesn't want to run into Jaffar. "I'm sorry. I wasn't thinking."

"That's okay. How about my place?"

I've never been to a friend's house before. I call my mom's phone and leave a message. I hope she's okay with it. She needs to be. I'm going anyway.

The bus ride to Mia's stop is uneventful. Kyle sits in the back, probably wanting to avoid another fight with Mia and a trip to the office. As we walk to her house, Mia tells me what happened in Principal Willems's office that morning. How Kyle blatantly lied. How Willems didn't take her seriously when she showed him the note. No wonder she's angry. I agree the note-writer is probably Kyle, but I wonder aloud, "Could it be Samantha?"

"I don't think so," Mia says. "You didn't see the way Kyle looked at me in the office. Like he wanted to rip my head off."

I know it's wrong to hate, but I hate Kyle. I hate Samantha and Rachel and Melody. I hate every person who's ever laughed at me, tripped me, thrown pencils at me. And I hate every person who's ever witnessed the bullying and never tried to stop it. I know I should find a place in my heart for understanding, for forgiveness. But I can't.

I glance at the houses we're walking past. I've never been in this neighborhood before. The gently arching trees make it feel quiet, peaceful. Life would be perfect if I could stay home all day and not worry about going to school. But that's not going to happen.

Mia stops at a blue house with flowers in the front. I follow her down the curving cement walkway.

Like everyone, her grandmother stares too long at my hijab when Mia introduces us. As Mia leads me to her bedroom, I notice two crosses on the fireplace mantel. I wonder if Jaffar saw them. I wonder if they gave him the same uneasy feeling I have right now. Of not belonging.

Mia sits on her bed. I look around her

room. It seems too frilly, with lace curtains and flowery wallpaper.

"It's the guest room," Mia says. "In case you're wondering."

I nod. "Won't your grandmother let you redecorate?"

Mia picks up a pillow and tugs at a lacy corner. "She's suggested it a few times. But I don't want her to go to the expense. I'm not sure how long I'll be here."

"Really?" I've known Mia for such a short time, yet my heart freezes at the thought of her leaving. "So … what does that depend on?"

"A few things." Then she says, "Do you want to do homework?"

I wish she would share more about her life. But she's obviously not ready. "Instead of homework," I say, "I'm wondering if you might show me some online sites."

"Nasreen." She tosses the pillow on the floor. "I thought you stopped reading that crap."

"Not reading. I have a different purpose in mind."

She stares at me. "Fine." Grabbing her laptop off her desk, she sits on the floor with her back against her bed. She's opening a site as I sit next to her. "This one is really popular," she says. "People post photos. Then readers comment. There are a few sites like this."

"Is it easy to open an account?"

"Yeah." She looks at me. "You mean right now?"

"Yes. Please." As Mia opens the new-account screen, I blurt out, "Not my real name!"

She gives me a crooked smile. "Okay."

"I'm thinking … Bad Girl."

She laughs. "Are you kidding me?"

I shake my head.

She thinks about it. "How about *Bad-Girlz*? I mean, if you're looking for a partner."

I smile. "Excellent." Part of me knows what we're doing shouldn't be fun. But it's improved Mia's mood. And seeing her happy makes me happy.

She types in all of the information. We pick out a dark background color that fits with our online persona. She asks, "Do you have anything to upload?"

"Not yet."

Then Mia says, "I have another idea." She backs out of that site and opens a webmail service page. She starts a new account under the name *BadGirlz*. "Do you still have that text about the online poll?"

I get out my phone. "What are you doing?"

"It's a trick I learned from one of my mom's boyfriends. A sleazy computer geek. You send texts from your computer instead of your phone. That way your phone number stays private."

I'm curious why anyone would need a trick like that. But I suppose *sleazy* says a lot. She double-checks her phone. Wants to verify the *Fidodish* e-mail address. Mia looks over at me. "What should we say?"

I feel a sudden twinge of guilt. But then I remember all of the times someone has called me raghead. Cow. Bitch. I recall the online messages saying I don't belong here. That I don't deserve to live. Kyle calling me Nasty Nasreen. Making sexual remarks. Trying to throw my Koran off the bus. In my mind, I see all of the disgusting comments people left on that poll.

Compared to all of that, what I'm doing is nothing. I just want to feel in control again. Something I haven't felt in a very long time.

Mia

It's not a good day to begin with. Then that note in my locker leaves me feeling shaken. I can deal with threats when I know who I'm up against. But this under-handed stuff is something else. How do I handle it? How do I protect myself?

In study hall, Nasreen suggests we get together after school. I'm miserable and not really in the mood to hang out. But I need to get my mind on other things, so I agree. Once we're in my room, she wants to go online. Fine. She wants my help opening a new account. Also fine. I'm so deep in my crap pile I don't question what she's doing.

Then it hits me. I can't believe it. Nasreen wants to bully the bullies. I laugh. I'm all for it. I'm so sick of what's going on that it doesn't bother me to give a little payback. If those idiots think it's fair game to play dirty tricks, they need to be prepared to get some in return.

We decide to text *Fidodish*, the idiot who sent us the link to the online poll. But when it comes to composing what to say, we both hesitate. I don't know what's going through Nasreen's head. But I'm thinking we're sinking to their level. Doesn't that make us idiots too? Then she gets this determined look in her eyes. Says, "I'd like to know who this is. Let's ask them to meet us somewhere. We can hide and check them out."

"Okay. Cool."

That's not bullying. It's looking for information. I type, *We have something you need to see. Meet us before first period.* I stop typing. Ask Nasreen, "Where?"

"Um. Somewhere there are lots of people, and it won't seem weird if they see us. How about 'top of the front steps'? And add 'urgent' after 'something.'"

I make the changes. Hover the cursor over Send. "Ready?"

Nasreen nods.

I tap the touchpad. Done.

We sit on the floor together, our backs against my bed. We're both quiet—lost in our own thoughts—when my computer *dings.* We both jump. I look at the screen. There's already an e-mail for *BadGirlz.* I tilt the laptop so Nasreen can read the screen too. The text from *Fidodish* reads:

Who are you?

"How should we respond?" Nasreen asks.

"We won't," I answer. "More mysterious that way."

She nods. As I close my laptop, she says, "You don't have to talk about it if you don't want to. I just want to say I'm sorry about what happened with Jaffar."

I lean my head against the bed. "Yeah."

"He shouldn't have asked you out in the first place."

"No, he shouldn't have."

"And I'm sorry you're so unhappy."

I turn my head and glance at her. Regardless of her online plans, there's a basic goodness to Nasreen I'm not used to. The people in my life have always looked out for themselves. They're nice when they think it will get them something. I've had information I've shared used against me. That's why I only trust people to a certain point. That's why I've been holding back on Nasreen. But I don't think I need to do that anymore.

"My mom's in prison," I say. "That's why I'm staying with my grandmother."

She nods.

"My mom's a scammer," I explain. "Always looking for a way to make money. This isn't the first time she got caught. This past Christmas, she used her boyfriend's credit card to the tune of a few thousand bucks. She didn't think he'd press charges but he did. The judge was sick of seeing her. Gave her a two-year sentence."

Nasreen lowers her chin. Stares at her hands. "I'm sorry. It must be hard for you to be separated from her."

I'm not sure what to say. If I tell the truth, I'll sound terrible. But I'm tired of lying. "Being apart from my mother is not entirely a bad thing."

Given how close her family is, I doubt she can understand this. But she nods. "Constant stress is never good. Even if the cause is someone you love."

"That's about the size of it." I smile. "Dude, you are very wise."

"No one has ever called me that before."

"Which, dude or wise?"

She laughs. "Either."

"Do you want to stay for dinner?" I ask.

"No, thank you. I'd better go home."

"Okay. I'll ask Gram if she can give you a lift." I set the laptop on the floor and get to my feet.

"Do you know how to drive?" Nasreen asks, looking up at me.

"No. Never needed to in the city."

"Driving would make our lives much easier."

"Except for the small problem of not having a car."

Nasreen sighs. "It seems there's a catch to every solution." She reaches up. I grab her hand and pull her to her feet.

That night I do homework until midnight. I hadn't realized I'd fallen so far behind. As I'm shoving my books into my backpack, I see the note from my locker. I take it out and read it again. *Bitch. I hate you. I'm going to kill you.* The nausea returns. The fear.

But this time I really think about it. Principal Willems said Kyle is popular, a model student. Model students don't kill other students. Unless they're total psychos. Kyle is a jerk and a half, but I don't think he's nuts.

If he wrote this note, he's messing with me. He wants to keep me off balance. Keep me looking over my shoulder. I can't fathom his reasoning. Maybe threatening people makes him feel manly. Maybe he's got problems at home, and the only time he feels powerful is preying on people weaker than him. Or maybe he was just born a douche bag.

I take a deep breath. If it's not Kyle, then who? The "Bitch. I hate you." fits for Samantha. But the threat doesn't. Nor does slipping the note in my locker—too big a chance she might get caught. When it occurs to me there might be an anonymous, racist wacko at Arondale High, a knot ties in my stomach.

Padding through the darkened house, I stop in the kitchen. Pull open a drawer. Pick out one of Gram's knives. The blade is the length of my hand. Big enough to defend myself. Small enough to slip in a pocket inside my backpack. Having a knife on campus could get me suspended. Or worse. But I'd rather be suspended and alive than suspended and dead. I carry the knife to my bedroom.

Nasreen

There's only one good thing about fights on the bus. They calm things down for a few days. Samantha and her friends are very quiet Tuesday morning. Kyle scowls at me from the aisle as he approaches. But he keeps walking and sits farther in the back like he did yesterday afternoon.

Mia looks much more relaxed when she gets on at her stop. I was shocked when she said her mother was in prison. But I'm glad she felt comfortable telling me. She's trusting me more. It's as though we've passed a hurdle in our friendship. It's strange that I went without a friend for so long. Now I can't imagine my life without one.

She sits next to me and whispers, "Ready for the big reveal?"

"I think so. But what if someone catches us? Or sees the guilt on our faces?"

She smiles. "Don't look guilty."

We get off the bus, and I quickly glance at the top step. Students are walking into the building. Some are standing around, chatting. We go inside.

"This way," Mia murmurs. I follow her to the bulletin board near the office. She says, "Watch for *Fidodish* while I peruse the news."

I feel like a secret agent as I casually lean against the wall next to the bulletin board. My stomach flutters with nerves. I peer through the open front entrance and the tall side windows.

"There's a Spanish Club meeting this

afternoon," Mia says. "Ooh, a basketball pep rally on Friday. Go, Arondale Yellow Jackets."

As Mia continues reciting the posted announcements, I see someone standing alone on the top step. He's glancing around as if looking for someone. I suck in a breath. "I don't believe it."

"What?" Mia says, casually turning. She gasps. "Are you kidding me? He's in our calculus class."

"Yes. Melvin Cho."

By now, Melvin is bouncing on his toes. He rubs the back of his neck, clearly nervous. I exchange a glance with Mia. "Now what?" I ask.

She shakes her head. "Not a clue." The first bell rings. "At least we know who *Fidodish* is." She shifts her backpack on her shoulder. "Guess I'll see you in calculus."

She leaves, but I stay rooted to the floor, my eyes on Melvin. I'm trying to make sense of this. He glances around one last time before coming through the front door. My nervous stomach has been replaced with confusion. Anger. Was he involved in that poll? It doesn't seem possible. He's never teased me. He's never been unkind.

I need to get to chemistry. We have a quiz this morning. Instead, I quickly catch up with him. "Are you *Fidodish*?" I ask bluntly.

He slows his pace and looks over. "*You* sent me that text yesterday?" He faces forward. "Oh, I get it. You wanted to find out who I am?"

"Did you create that online poll?" I ask.

"Me? No! Of course not." He takes a deep breath. "I just wanted to warn you."

Then it dawns on me how he got our phone numbers. Mr. Humphrey has us exchange them for calculus study groups.

Melvin continues, "I monitor the Aron-dale jerks. Samantha started that poll."

"But you call yourself *Fidodish*. That's so ... crude."

"So? It helps me fit in. *Future bio-chemist* might be a little too revealing, don't you think?"

He's right, of course. That's why Mia and I are *BadGirlz*.

He stops in front of a classroom. "I have to go." He leans in and whispers, "Just to let you know, this has been a little proj-ect of mine for a while. I have all of their online aliases. All of their phone numbers." He gives me an evil grin. "I'm happy to share." He disappears inside.

The late bell rings. I rush to chemistry.

The morning goes by in a blur. I make sure I get to third period early. The second Melvin slides into his seat, I'm standing next to him. "I'd like that list," I whisper.

He nods. "I'll send it to your e-mail."

I return to my desk. Mia comes in just as the bell rings. "Having a good morning?" she asks.

"So far." I smile as a tiny sense of control washes over me.

During lunch, I tell Mia about Melvin's list.

"What's your plan?" she asks, taking a bite of her sandwich.

"I'm not sure."

"Well, what's your ultimate goal? Pain? Embarrassment? Fear?"

Hearing her spell it out like that makes me uneasy. But it only takes a second to get over my discomfort. "All of the above." I look at Mia. "What about you?"

She swallows. "Wiping that smirk off Kyle's smug-ass face would be a great start."

I open my container of leftovers. Lentil casserole is my favorite. But most of it goes uneaten. My stomach is rolling with anticipation.

In my bedroom that night, I force myself to finish my homework before I go online. It's after eleven when I finally open the *BadGirlz* e-mail account. There's a message in the Sent folder, sent to a phone number. Mia must have sent a text. I open the message. I'll have to ask her about it tomorrow, because it doesn't make much sense.

In the inbox is the e-mail from *Fidod-ish* with an attachment. I open it. It's Melvin's list of names and phone numbers, along with online aliases. Samantha, Melody, Rachel, and Kyle are all there. Plus a lot of other kids from Arondale High. It's unsettling to attach real names to the hateful online comments they wrote about me on that poll.

I take a deep breath. One by one, I

enter and save their phone numbers into the address book. I decide to start small. I overheard that Samantha is dating a guy from a different school. I address a text message to her phone number. Then I type:

Thought u should know. Saw Rachel with your BF. They looked cozy.

I press Send before I change my mind. It's less than a minute before I get a reply:

What? Who the f are u?

I write back:

Someone who hates seeing friends screw over friends.

It's not me who quickly clicks Send. It's *BadGirlz*. And *BadGirlz* closes her computer wishing she could see the confused and hurt look on Samantha's face.

CHAPTER 20

Mia

As soon as I get home Tuesday, I open
Melvin's e-mail attachment. Wow. So
many names. So many phone numbers
and online accounts. He's a geek after my
own heart. I have an overabundance of
riches and don't know where to start. But I
quickly come up with an idea.

I go to one of Kyle's online sites.
He uses the alias *Bonger*. His avatar is a
hookah. He obviously likes his smoke.
He's downloaded lots of photos, mostly
drug-related. There are even a couple of
him partying—puffing on joints. What
an idiot. Doesn't he realize everyone in

the world has access to these images?
That employers and colleges will probably
Google him?

I open up a new account under the
name *BadGirlz*. I leave the comment:

You're an ass wipe, Kyle Spencer. Lamest
site ever.

Yeah, my comment is lame too. But
revealing his real name to the world feels
awesome. And I'm just getting started.

Using our *BadGirlz* e-mail account, I
send a text to Kyle's phone:

Watch your back, bong boy. I'm after you.

He doesn't text back. I hope that
means I've confused him. Thrown him off
balance.

On the bus the next morning, Nasreen
and I quietly compare online notes. She's
focusing on Samantha. I'm squarely cen-
tered on Kyle. For the next stage of my
plan, I'm going to need a guy's help.

I get to calculus early and wait for Melvin. He's soon gliding into the classroom. I've never really checked him out before. He's not bad looking. Medium height. Lithe body. His hair is that nice combination of neat and floppy. As soon as he's in his seat, I'm crouching next to his desk. "Thanks for the list," I whisper.

"You're welcome," he whispers back.

"I assume you dislike the people on it as much as we do."

"I'd say that's a yes."

"I have a proposition." As I quickly explain what I want, a grin spreads across his face.

He says, "It won't be easy, but I'll see what I can do."

"Thanks." I tap his desk and whisper, "You have nice hair."

I laugh as he instinctively runs his fingers through his hair. He looks back at me with a sly grin.

"What's that all about?" Nasreen asks when I'm back at my desk.

"Just a little revenge of the nerds."

Before class ends, Mr. Humphrey announces, "Remember, AP exams are coming up in May." He writes the dates on the board. "This is what it's all about, folks. Be prepared."

It's only March, but my pulse quickens. I hope I'll be ready by then. Nasreen and I share a glance. I can tell she's nervous too. School would be so much easier if we could simply focus on our work. Dealing with the Samanthas and Kyles of the world is a major distraction. I mean, I'm carrying a friggin' knife in my backpack. I want to finally be done with this.

The bell rings. Though I'm not very hungry, I can use the break. I gather my things. Nasreen lingers at her desk.

"Coming to lunch?" I ask.

"Yes," she says, slowly getting to her feet.

As we make our way down the hallway, I understand why she wanted to wait. We're behind Samantha's crew for once, instead of in front of them. The three of them usually walk so close together, they're like a single body with three heads. But today Rachel trails behind. Samantha turns and glares at her. Says something I can't hear. But I can see her cheeks are an angry red. Rachel abruptly stops walking. She slowly follows them into the lunchroom.

"It looks like all is not well in Sammyland," I say. "Your online trick worked."

I expect Nasreen to cheer, gloat, give me a high-five. But she only manages a tight smile.

We continue to our lunch spot. Nasreen seems a million miles away. I know what it's like to need space. So I don't bug her. Don't ask questions. I just hope she's not coming apart at the seams.

We're supposed to turn our phones off in all of our classes. The rest of the day I turn mine to vibrate and stuff it deep in my backpack. In study hall, I just barely hear it hum. I pull my backpack onto my lap and act like I'm searching for a pen. I look at the screen. It's a text from Melvin.

> Had to pull big favor to get this. U owe me. :)

He's sent me a photo. Holy crap. It's of Kyle in the gym shower. He's naked, facing the camera. You can see *everything*. I quickly lower my backpack to the floor. Press my hand over my mouth to hide my huge smile. Nasreen looks over. I shake my head. "Later," I whisper.

When the bell rings, I show her the photo.

"Oh." She blushes and covers her eyes with her hand. "What are you going to do with it?"

"End Kyle's bullying forever." At first I wonder if I should wait and do this from the *BadGirlz* e-mail account. Then I realize I don't care if Kyle has my phone number. I *want* him to know it's from me. Using Kyle's number from Melvin's list, I send him the photo along with the text:

> Leave me and Nasreen alone. Or I release this photo EVERYWHERE.

We're still at our desks when I get a text from Kyle a few seconds later:

> That includes phone and online! Or everyone is gonna find out ALL about you. One more written, verbal, or physical insult and photo goes viral.

After school, Kyle is leaning against the side of the bus, his arms crossed. His gaze is blistering. If he put that note in my locker, maybe this is when he carries out his threat. Maybe he has a switchblade in his pocket. I shift my backpack to one shoulder. Unzip it slightly so I can reach my knife if I have to.

My heart is racing. My breathing turns shallow. I consider not taking the bus and walking the five miles home. But I need to show him I'm not afraid. That he can't threaten us anymore.

Nasreen slows in front of me. I'm sure she sees him too. "Keep going," I whisper. "I'll handle this."

We climb the steps into the bus. Kyle slips in behind me. He doesn't say anything. But I feel hatred billowing off him. I reach into my backpack. Touch the smooth hilt of the knife.

He's so close now I can feel his breath

against my ear. I stop. Twist around. "Back off."

His mouth screws up. He hesitates. I can tell he's thinking about that picture.

"I said, *back off.* Or I'll do what I promised."

He steps back an inch.

"And don't sit anywhere near us again. Ever."

Nasreen and I find a seat in the middle of the bus. Kyle passes us and keeps going. I take a deep breath and let it out. Quickly zip up my pack. It's a long time before I'm breathing normally again.

Nasreen

Mia shows me her phone in study hall Wednesday afternoon. It's a photo of Kyle. He's completely naked! Mia says he won't be bothering us again. She's blackmailing him. I should feel ashamed. But I don't. I'm glad. I should feel ashamed for causing a rift between Samantha and Rachel. But if I have any remorse, it must be deeply buried, because I feel only satisfaction. I've been suffering at their hands since middle school. I'm a bottomless pit of frustration and anger.

As soon as I get home, I go online. I open the networking site where Mia created an account for us. I read the directions for starting a poll. I start a new one titled *The Biggest Sluts at Arondale High*. I begin the list with three names: Samantha, Melody, and Rachel. Then, using the *BadGirlz* e-mail, I send texts to every phone number I entered into the address book:

> Cool poll. Check it out.

Over the next hour, I watch the crude comments mount. People add names to the poll. No one seems to care who they're attacking, as long as it's not them.

A text arrives for *BadGirlz*. It's from Samantha:

> I'll find you out bitch.

I text back:

> Go ahead and try, Top Slut. This will just get worse.

"Nasreen!" Mom calls. "Come help with dinner."

I close the laptop. Make my way to the kitchen. I barely pay attention as I chop vegetables. My mind is far away with *Bad-Girlz* plots and plans.

"You're very quiet," Mom says. She fills a pot with water. "What's wrong?"

"Nothing," I answer.

I feel her staring at me. What would she say if she knew my alter ego is planning a fake party? That tonight she's going to invite half of those assholes and not the other half. That she's going to watch as the rejects find out what it's like to be excluded.

I climb onto the bus the next morning, my shoulders back, head high. I'm feeling so brave I look at the back seat, right at Samantha.

"What are you staring at, raghead?" she says.

I slide into my seat. She can call me whatever she wants. With the poll, now she knows what it's like to feel humiliated. That makes us a tiny bit more even. And if her bullying gets worse, I'll find a way to embarrass her more. I'll take a photo. Like the one Melvin got of Kyle. She'll be sorry.

Then Samantha yells, "Hey, *BadGirlz*!"

I almost turn my head. Does she know? No, of course not. How could she? She's testing me. I stare straight ahead.

Kyle gets on at his stop. He doesn't sit close. I hear him talking in the back. Then I hear Samantha. The bus starts moving again. Are they talking about me? Comparing notes? I knot my fingers in my lap.

I'm relieved when Mia gets on.

"Hi," I say. My voice is hard. I'm beginning to panic. I'm afraid to move.

"What's up?" she asks.

A number of people in the back yell,

"Hey, *BadGirlz!*" I recognize Samantha's voice. Kyle's. A few others.

I feel Mia stiffen. She leans in and whispers, "They don't know anything. They're guessing."

I nod, hoping she's right. Praying she's right.

The bus is quiet the rest of the way to school. I'm not sure if that's good or bad. Does it mean they've given up?

The bus stops and we quickly get off. Before we separate, Mia says, "Remember, they don't know a thing. So act normal."

Normal? I'm not sure what that is anymore. Cowering Nasreen or vengeful *Bad-Girlz*? I feel sweat prickling under my hijab. What will they do if they discover it's me? They'll retaliate. It will be horrible. I've got to calm down.

I take a deep breath as I make my way to my locker. As I turn the combination,

I repeat to myself, *They don't know. They don't know.* I've just opened the door when a hand slams it shut. I twist around. It's Samantha, wearing the same scowl as Rachel and Melody standing next to her.

"Your scarf is wet," Samantha says. "Why are you sweating?"

I try to meet her eyes. To be fierce. Then I wonder if that's normal. "I have to get to class," I say, turning back to my locker. I start my combination again.

"We figured it out, you know," Samantha says.

A shiver of fear runs down my back. My hand shakes. *She's lying. They don't know.*

"You and your girlfriend are *BadGirlz*. You lied about Rachel. You started that poll."

I finally get my locker open. Murmur, "I don't know what you're talking about."

"And now there's a spectacular party

you're inviting only *some* of us to? What's up with that?"

"It's rude," Rachel says.

I exchange books between my backpack and locker. Close it. "I have to get to class."

Samantha shoves my shoulder hard. My locker bangs as I slam against it. I want to cry out, but my heart is lodged in my throat.

"You're *BadGirlz*. Just admit it."

I stare into Samantha's eyes. Into those hate-filled eyes. My frustration fizzes up. All of that bottled-up anger. I can't hold it in another second.

"Yes!" I shout. "And you deserve it! All of it!" I look at the three of them. "You're cruel. Why are you so cruel to people?"

Samantha raises her fist. "No one messes with me, raghead. Get it? No one."

To my right I hear, "Yeah, I get it."

CHAPTER 22

Mia

I'm just leaving my locker when I hear a metallic bang. Then yelling. I'm too far away to recognize voices. But a hunch tells me it's Nasreen. And if it's Nasreen, this cannot be good.

I run down the hallway. Push through the crowd going in the opposite direction. I see Samantha's raised fist. Nasreen pressed up against the lockers. I stop thinking and operate on instinct. Unzipping my backpack, I pull out the kitchen knife. Drop my pack on the floor. Take a defensive stance—feet spread, hands out to my sides.

"Back off," I say, trying to keep my voice flat. Even. Meaning business.

Melody shrieks when she sees the knife. The three of them immediately step away from Nasreen. She's staring at the knife too. Her eyes are wide. Shocked.

"What are you doing?" Samantha says. Her eyes flash from my face to the knife and back again. "Are you crazy?"

"Go!" I say. "Leave us alone."

"Lower that knife! Right now!" It's a man's voice. An authoritative voice. Principal Willems is trotting toward us, along with the custodian who doubles as a security guard. Crap.

They stop an arm's length away. Willems tentatively holds out his hand. "Give me the weapon, Mia."

Weapon. It's not a weapon, I want to tell him. *It's a kitchen knife.* But I suddenly see myself as he must see me. A dangerous, raving black girl from the inner city. "It's not what you think." I hand him the knife by the handle. "I only wanted to scare them. They were threatening Nasreen."

Willems carefully passes the knife to the custodian. Then he eyes the gawking students milling around. "Everyone get to class. Now!" Samantha and her friends start to slip into the crowd. "Wait. Not you three." Then he says, "I want all of you in the office this minute."

Nasreen and I sit in the outer office while the principal meets with Samantha, Rachel, and Melody. He told us not to talk. The school secretary is keeping a sharp eye on us, making sure we follow his directions. I keep looking at Nasreen, wanting some sign that she's okay. That I did the right thing. But she's leaning forward, focused on the floor. Pressing her hands against the seat of her chair. Like she might throw up.

After about fifteen minutes, the three come out and sit. Principal Willems crooks his finger at Nasreen. She gets up and follows him into his office. Her eyes are downcast the whole time.

I feel like I failed her. I saw the look in her eyes when she saw the knife. Like she didn't know me. Like I terrified her. Like I really was crazy.

I don't know. Maybe I am crazy. Just like my mom. A loser. A screw-up. Always one step away from ruining my life. I wrap my arms around my stomach. My head buzzes. I'm not her. I am *not* her. But here I am, in big trouble. I suddenly wonder if this is why I don't want to visit her in prison. I don't want to see my future.

Nasreen leaves after ten minutes in Willems's office. I automatically get to my feet. She still hasn't looked at me. I could really use a friend right now. I'm afraid I've lost her.

I sit stiffly in front of Willems's desk. He folds his hands on top of some papers. Clears his throat. "First of all, because you had a weapon, I'm required to contact the police. Which I've done."

I nod.

He says, "Tell me what happened."

Since I can't lose a thing by telling the truth, I honestly describe what I heard, what I saw, what I did. I explain why I had the knife in the first place—because of that threatening note in my locker.

He doesn't interrupt me. When I'm done talking, he says, "Do you understand what poor judgment you showed, bringing a weapon to school? And then threatening other students?"

"I just wanted to scare them."

"You had other options. Why didn't you get an adult? A teacher? Someone from the office?"

"I didn't have time. Samantha was about to hit Nasreen. And I tried before ..." my voice trails off.

He sits there a minute, staring at me. I squirm a little but look back at him. He picks up the phone. Punches in some numbers. "Sergeant? This is Principal Willems. We won't be needing the squad car." Pause. "Yes, I'm sure. We'll handle this internally." He hangs up.

He looks at me again. "Your story matches Nasreen's. And I'm inclined to believe you. But there are consequences for having that knife. I'm suspending you for ten days. Then I'm recommending to the school board that you be expelled for the rest of the year."

"What?" I feel my jaw drop.

"Would you rather go to jail?"

"No! But ... what about school? My classes?"

"You can attend private school or be homeschooled. Or request admittance to another public school. And you have the right to appeal the board's decision."

There's a knock at the door. The secretary pokes her head in. "Mia's grandmother is on her way. So are the other girls' parents."

My heart sinks even farther. Gram. She can't handle this. It will kill her. I'm going to foster care for sure.

The custodian/security guard walks me to my locker. All I have in there are books. I quickly stuff them into my backpack. I want to get this over with before first period lets out. I can't stomach everyone in school watching me.

On the drive home, Gram asks me what happened. Willems already told her the worst of it. So I tell her everything else. About the bullying. About getting sick of the bullying and trying to help Nasreen.

"I wish you'd told me about all this," she says.

"I was going to. But I didn't think you'd understand."

She shakes her head. "I raised your mother, didn't I? I'm very familiar with principal's offices."

I hadn't thought about that.

"I'm stronger than you think, Mia. I know more than you think." She stops at a red light. "I'm not weak. I'm sad. There's a big difference."

"What are you sad about?" I ask.

The light changes, and she presses the gas pedal. "Your mother. How much of her sorry life is my fault. About waiting so long to be a part of your life. Wondering if I'll make the same mistakes with you."

I'm quiet as I digest that information. Then I ask, "Are you going to send me to foster care?"

"No." She glances over at me. "Honestly, I might have answered differently a few weeks ago. But when I got that call from the school office today, I was terrified something terrible had happened. I'm relieved you're all right." Then she says, "You're not your mother, Mia. I'm not the same person I was when I raised her. We'll make this work."

She pulls into our driveway. "And I'm going to stop bugging you about seeing her. If and when you're ready, let me know." She stops the car and turns off the ignition. "Okay?"

"Yeah," I say.

She pats my hands and squeezes my fingers. I squeeze back.

Nasreen

I'm preparing myself for Samantha's attack when Mia arrives. I could cry with relief. Then I see the knife in her hand. I suck in my breath. What is she going to do? Then everything blurs.

The next thing I know, I'm sitting outside the principal's office. I feel sick to my stomach. Mia's here with me, but I can't meet her eyes. I'm too ashamed. Too angry with myself. This was not her fault. It was mine. She was trying to defend me. She's in horrible trouble right now because of me. She must hate me.

When Willems calls me into his office,

I describe what happened. Then, because I have nothing to lose, I tell him about all of the bullying. I tell him about Samantha and Kyle tormenting us at school and on the bus. About the online polls and ugly comments. I leave out any mention of Melvin.

He listens. Then he says, "Unfortunately, what happens online is out of the school's control. But what happens on campus and on the bus is. Why didn't you report this sooner?"

"Mia and I almost spoke to the counselor. But Samantha threatened us. I was afraid."

"Okay," he says. "Thank you, Nasreen. I'll look into what you've told me." Then he says, "I'd like you to see Mr. Clarke anyway. There are some coping skills he can teach you."

I'm not sure I'll do this, but I nod.

He stands up and escorts me out.

I pass Mia, but I still can't look at her. More than anything, I want to hug her. To thank her for defending me. For being such a good friend. But at the moment, I'm sure she wishes she'd never met me.

I don't see Mia in calculus, so I assume she's been suspended. When Samantha and her friends also aren't on the bus that afternoon, I figure Willems suspended them too. Someone sits next to me. It's Allie Silva. We share the same English class. She smiles. "Hi. Sorry about your friend."

I nod. "Thank you."

I'm glad someone friendly is sitting next to me. But I don't know what else to say. I keep wondering what happened to Mia. I hope she's all right. I hope she forgives me one day.

Since I wasn't in trouble, Principal Willems didn't call my parents. They don't know what happened. Mom is at the kitchen table when I walk in. My throat closes up. The last time I spoke to her about bullying, she didn't understand. But I'm tired of being afraid all the time. I'm sick of worrying about what other people think about me, even my parents. I picture Mia. How brave she could be. How she could stand up to anyone.

"Mom?" I whisper.

She looks up from the magazine she's reading.

"There's something I need to tell you. It's really important."

By the time I'm finished, her eyes have glazed over. I still don't think she gets what's going on. But I feel better just telling her. I end with, "And I'm going to see the school counselor tomorrow." I don't realize it's something I've decided until it's out of my mouth.

She looks taken aback. "Why?"

"Because I need help dealing with these bullies."

Her eyes narrow. "I don't want you talking about the family with a stranger."

"I won't talk about the family."

"We should discuss this with your father."

"No, Mom. This is something I need to do."

She gives me a sideways look. Then she takes a deep breath. "Fine."

"And … I'd like to find a different way to school. Catch a ride with a student."

She shakes her head. "No, absolutely not. I don't trust young drivers."

I say, "Okay." But I'm not going to give up on the idea.

On the way to my room, I hear music coming from behind Jaffar's door. I knock.

"What?"

I turn the knob and step inside. He's sitting at his desk, staring at his computer.

"I'd like your help with Mom and Dad."

He doesn't respond. I continue talking to his back. "I'd like you to tell them that not all teen drivers are reckless. Melvin Cho from my calculus class said he's started driving to school. He doesn't live far from us."

Jaffar shrugs.

I suddenly realize how much of a bully my brother can be. "Jaffar!" I say. "You are so rude! And what you did to Mia was thoughtless. I hope you're ashamed." As I leave I add, "And have you ever heard of earphones?" I slam his door on my way out.

Once in my room, I fish my phone out of my backpack. I'm desperate to talk to Mia. I start to press her number, then stop. She's probably still angry. The last thing I want is to make her more upset. I'll let her contact me when she's ready.

In her honor, I open my laptop and go

online. I delete my Facebook page. Then I get rid of the link to the poll Samantha started about me. I won't look at it again, just like Mia suggested. Then I delete the *BadGirlz* accounts.

I see the counselor, Mr. Clarke, the next day. He listens. He says I started out being too passive. Then I jumped to being too aggressive. He says the best way to deal with bullies is to be assertive. Make eye contact. Stand straight. Act confident. I recognize Mia in some of his explanations.

Then he says, "When young people get away with bullying, it tends to get worse. Sometimes bullies are the most respected kids in school. They have status." The bell rings, and he stands. "If the bullying gets worse, tell me or Principal Willems. Don't hesitate, okay? We'll deal with it."

"When will Samantha be back?" I ask, gathering my things. "And Mia?"

"The school policy for bullying is a two-week suspension. Mia will likely be expelled for having a weapon."

"Expelled! But … she was defending me."

His eyes soften. "I'm sorry. I know she is your friend." As I leave his office, he says, "Just to let you know, I'm pushing for changes in school policy. I think it's time for Arondale to deal with bullying in a different way."

I walk down the hallway, unsure what to think. I'm worried about Mia. I'm also worried what will happen when Samantha returns. I feel a little better knowing I have adults I can talk to if something bad happens. But that's after the fact. The counselor and principal aren't in my classes or guarding the hallways. They aren't everywhere, every second of the day. Teachers have their backs turned much of the time. In many ways, I'm still on my own. And whatever changes Mr. Clarke wants to make will not help me now.

During the following two weeks, I don't hear from Mia. I assume our friendship is over. I'm sure she regrets ever sitting next to me on the bus her first day.

The Monday Samantha returns, I see her sitting in her usual spot in the back of the bus. She stares at me but doesn't say anything when I get on at my stop. I assume this is because Principal Willems has put her on warning. At Kyle's stop, he still doesn't sit behind me. I think he's worried about the photo Mia will release if he harasses me. I wonder how long they'll behave.

In chemistry that morning, Mrs. Jamison is late again. A pencil flies wide of my hijab and lands on my desk. A few classmates laugh. "Hey. Sorry," Felicia says with mocking sincerity.

The old Nasreen is tempted to absorb the hatred and do nothing. *BadGirlz* imagines calling Felicia a bitch and throwing the pencil at her. The new Nasreen remembers Mr. Clarke's instructions. She rises from her desk. Looks Felicia square in the eyes. Sets the pencil on her desk. And says, "I think you dropped this."

Now that Samantha is back, I feel naked in the hallways without Mia. How did I ever do this without her? As Samantha glares at me before lunch, the memory of our fight sickens me. I want to speed up, lower my eyes, get away. But I force myself to slow down, walk normally, look back at her. She keeps glaring but doesn't say a word. They pass me. As I watch them get farther ahead, I notice there's still a knot in my stomach. It has nothing to do with fear. I take a deep breath and catch up with them. "Samantha," I say.

She turns.

"I'm sorry about the poll I started." I glance at Rachel. "And I'm sorry about the rumor."

I rush to my eating spot before they can respond. I'm not sure if apologizing was passive. I don't care. It was just something I needed to do.

CHAPTER 24

Mia

It's the first night of my suspension. Gram and I are at the kitchen table, talking about what I want to do. Whether I want to fight the expulsion or go to a new school. I hate the idea of defending myself in front of the school board. And, except for Nasreen, I don't have a lot of love for Arondale High.

"There's Saint Alban's," Gram says. "It's half a mile from here. I have some money. You could go until the end of the school year."

"A Catholic school? Do they wear uniforms?"

"I believe so."

I think about it. On the upside, it would be close enough to walk. That means no bus. No jerks on the bus. "I hate wasting your money," I say.

"Let me worry if it's a waste or not."

I sigh. "Okay. St. Alban's."

"Good. We'll go tomorrow. See if we can get you enrolled."

She rises from the table.

"Gram?" I wait until she's looking at me. "Thanks for this. And for letting me stay. I'm sorry I screwed up."

She studies my face with a squint. "I see some of your mother in you. In your eyes. Your chin. Otherwise, you're nothing alike. Partying was more important to her than studying. I doubt she even knew what AP meant." She taps the table. "You acted impulsively without thinking it through. Will you do that again?"

"No. No way."

"You're not a screw-up, Mia."

I appreciate her support. But I'm not sure I believe it. "This expulsion will go on my record. I won't get into a good college. I won't get scholarships."

"How much do you want to go to college?" she asks.

"A lot. It's … everything."

"Will you let this get in your way?"

I take a deep breath. "No."

She smiles.

I start St. Alban's the following Monday. Wearing a uniform sucks. But at least it helps me fit in. Makes me feel a little more like everyone else. I'm doing my usual thing of laying low. Scoping out the territory. Being a serious student. No one's insulted me yet. But it's just the first day. I'm sure the bullies are lurking here, like they're lurking everywhere. If they make themselves known, I'll deal with them. Without weaponry, of course.

After a couple of weeks, I'm falling into the routine of St. Alban's. I'm daringly not buttoning the top of my white shirt. I figure I've got to show some individuality. I've been talking to a few kids. They're okay. Nice, I guess. But there's no one here I'm connecting with like I connected with Nasreen. There are so many times I've picked up the phone to call her, then changed my mind. The fact is she hasn't called me either. Which tells me she'd rather not communicate. I can't blame her.

I really start thinking about Nasreen as the AP exam gets closer. It's a Thursday night, four weeks after I was expelled. I'm struggling with a ridiculously hard calculus problem. I grab my phone. Quickly press her number before I change my mind.

She answers with, "Mia?" She doesn't sound angry. Just … tentative.

"Hey," I say back. "How's it going?"

"Okay. How are you?"

"I'm fine. Is … is it okay that I called? Because I can hang up—"

"Yes!" she shouts. "I mean, no, don't hang up. I've been wanting to talk to you since … well, since that day."

"Why didn't you?"

"I got you into trouble. You must hate me."

"I don't hate you. I got myself into trouble. I thought you hated me for scaring the crap out of you."

"No!" She's quiet a few seconds. "I'm sorry for the misunderstanding."

"Yeah." Then I say, "I'm having calculus issues."

She sighs. "So am I."

"Do you want to come over and study? This weekend? It will have to be

Sunday, though. I'm visiting my mom on Saturday."

"Yes." I can hear the relief in her voice. "I would love to come over."

"You won't recognize the place," I say, glancing around my room. "I've done a little decorating. The lace curtains and pillows are gone."

"So you're planning on staying for a while?"

"Yep. Maybe back to Arondale High in the fall. I haven't decided."

"Oh, please come back! I'm working on my parents to let me ride with Melvin Cho. And Allie, a girl from my English class, has started driving too. I'm sure they'd take both of us. No more bus."

"Awesome." Then I ask, "Is the bullying still bad?"

She doesn't answer for moment. Finally she says, "In some ways it's the same. Mostly it's better. The best thing is

that I have friends now, Mia. I'm happier.
And I have you to thank for that."

"Me?"

"Allie always thought I wanted to be
left alone. But when you and I became
friends, she realized that wasn't true.
Melvin has been nicer to me too. It's like
kids were afraid to talk to me, and now
they aren't. I'm almost cool. In an uncool
kind of way."

I laugh.

"I'm glad you called," Nasreen says. "I
miss you."

"Yeah. I miss you too."

Nasreen

In some ways, I prefer eating lunch outside. But the wall near the soccer field is too small and awkward for five people. The first week of senior year we find an empty table in the lunchroom. Mia is sitting next to me, eating pizza. Melvin is next to Allie. Another student, Jacob, has joined us.

I look around furtively. Even being here with friends, the lunchroom makes me nervous. I feel like a mouse being watched by many hungry cats. It doesn't take long for one to pounce.

"Losers." Elliott Adams laughs as he walks by our table. One of his friends shoves Melvin's tray. It almost topples into his lap.

I set down my sandwich as kids at other tables join in the laughter. The familiar knot ties in my stomach.

Mia eyes me. "Jerks," she says in her unflappable way.

I give her a small smile.

She takes another bite of pizza and a makes a face. "Okay, that's it. I'm switching to meatloaf tomorrow."

Melvin looks at me after righting his tray. "Don't worry, Nasreen. In a few years you'll have an amazing career. Those idiots will be flipping burgers. If they're lucky."

"Hey, maybe we'll even be their bosses," Allie says.

I take a deep breath and pick up my sandwich again. "I'm not sure I would like that." Then I grin and say, "But it's not an unpleasant thought either."

Mia raises her juice carton. "Here's to the losers' table."

We all tap our drinks together. "The losers' table," we say in unison.

It feels good to joke. It feels good to have friends to joke with. Yet it doesn't seem right. I shouldn't need friends to feel safe at school. I shouldn't have to feel nervous every time I go online or read a text. Everything has changed. Nothing has changed.

Friday morning I sit with Mia during the first school assembly. I'm expecting the usual announcements, followed by the usual pep rally. At first, I don't pay much attention to Mr. Willems's speech. Then he pauses and looks out over the student body. It feels like his eyes linger on me when he clears his throat. "The level of

bullying at AHS saddens me. It's unacceptable," he says. "We've put in place a
new anti-bullying program."

He describes the program. Students
who bully will have to take action to stop
bullying at school. Part of their "training"
will be hearing how they've hurt other
students. Mia and I exchange a look. I
wonder if my eyes have grown as wide as
hers.

Mia

My first day of senior year is as nerve-racking as the day I started at Arondale. Only this time it's not my skin color catching attention. It's my reputation. I'm the wacko who got expelled for waving a knife around. Kids stare. They whisper. They also give me some distance. That's not necessarily a bad thing. But I see myself through their eyes. With all of the violence happening at schools these days, I understand why I make them nervous. Guess I need to show everyone my warm and fuzzy side this year.

During the summer, I almost decided

to stay at St. Alban's. Gram said she had enough money for two more semesters. It was Mom who helped me choose. She sat across from me in her prison khakis looking a little too pale and thin but definitely calmer. Her blue eyes were clear and steady. She said, "What do *you* want?"

I thought about it. "Nasreen is a good friend. I'd like to spend my last year of high school with her."

"Then go to Arondale," Mom said. "Face your monsters. If I'd done more of that when I was younger, I might not be here now."

It's hard visiting Mom in prison. But I'm glad I go. It feels great to hug her. She's going to live with Gram and me when she gets out. I think they're both a lot different than they were fourteen years ago. Maybe we can make it work.

We have a school crew now. We're a bunch of misfits. I say that with affection.

It's nice having a group to eat lunch with. To hang out with. I've got my eyes on Melvin Cho. There's a fall dance coming up. I may drop a hint. Or maybe I'll hit him over the head, figuratively speaking. I have a hunch he's the needs-more-than-a-hint type.

At the first assembly of the school year, Principal Willems announces a new anti-bullying program. I guess any change is better than none. Except my experience with the principal has not been all that positive. I'm not sure I trust that his heart is in it. But then a strange thing happens.

Three weeks into the school year, Willems calls Nasreen and me into his office. He invites us to the first anti-bullying meeting. He wants us to describe our experiences being bullied. He must see the doubt in our eyes. The suspicion. "You don't have to answer right away," he says. "Think about it."

I do think about it. And it's not something I want to do. First, it feels a little racist. Like we're the school's token minorities. And I don't want to do Willems any favors. He did zilch about punishing Kyle last year.

"What have you decided?" I ask Nasreen that afternoon at lunch. I'm thinking there's no way she'll go through with it.

But she says, "How are people going to know what it's like unless we tell them?"

Okay. Good point. I give it more thought. Maybe this will be a way to face my monsters, like Mom said. And maybe I do owe Willems for not sending me to jail.

We walk into the classroom where the session is held. Principal Willems is standing to the side, his arms crossed. Mr. Clarke, the counselor, is in the front. He's explaining something, but I'm not really listening. I'm near the door with Nasreen, staring at ten Arondale students slouched in their seats, glaring at us. They've already been accused of bullying this year. One of them is Kyle. Another is Samantha. My heart thwacks in my chest.

I do not want to be here. This is not worth it. I look at Nasreen. Her face is pale. *Let's go*, I mouth.

But she grabs my hand. Squeezes it before walking to the front of the room. She holds her head high and takes a deep breath. "My name is Nasreen," she says. "I'm going to tell you how it feels to be me."

ABOUT THE AUTHOR

M. G. Higgins writes fiction and nonfiction for children and young adults. Her novel *Bi-Normal* won the 2013 Independent Publisher (IPPY) silver medal for Young Adult Fiction. Her novel *Falling Out of Place* was a 2013 Next Generation Indie Book Awards finalist and a 2014 Young Adult Library Services Association (YALSA) Quick Pick nominee.

Ms. Higgins's nearly thirty nonfiction titles range from science and technology to history and biographies. While her wide range of topics reflects her varied interests, she especially enjoys writing about mental health issues.

Before becoming a full-time writer, she worked as a school counselor and had a private counseling practice.

When she's not writing, Ms. Higgins enjoys hiking and taking photographs in the Arizona desert where she lives with her husband.